To Jenny,

Happy birthday.

God bless

[signature]

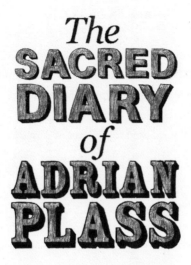

The SACRED DIARY of ADRIAN PLASS

Adrian Plass and the Church Weekend

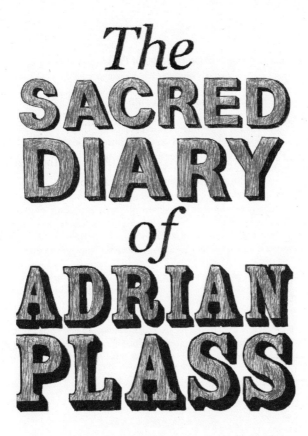

The SACRED DIARY of ADRIAN PLASS

Adrian Plass and the Church Weekend

HODDER &
STOUGHTON

First published in Great Britain in 2013 by Hodder & Stoughton
An Hachette UK company

1

A CIP catalogue record for this title is available from the British Library

ISBN 978 1 444 74544 3
eBook ISBN 978 1 444 74545 0

Typeset by Hewer Text UK Ltd, Edinburgh
Printed and bound by CPI Group (UK) Ltd, Croydon, CR0 4YY

Hodder & Stoughton policy is to use papers that are natural, renewable
and recyclable products and made from wood grown in sustainable
forests. The logging and manufacturing processes are expected to
conform to the environmental regulations of the country of origin.

Hodder & Stoughton Ltd
338 Euston Road
London NW1 3BH

www.hodderfaith.com

This book is dedicated to the resident and extended Community of Scargill House in North Yorkshire. Your love and affection over the last three years have enriched my life more than you will ever know.

Introduction

I used to think I would never write a funnier book than the first *Sacred Diary* – precisely because I was unlikely to experience such profound unhappiness again.

1985 had been a traumatic year. Frustration and acute unhappiness with myself, the Church and just about everything else culminated in a severe stress illness that was anything but funny for our family. Unable on health grounds to continue working with children in care, I spent most of my time in our upstairs sitting-room experimenting with the arduous but oddly therapeutic business of writing.

Coming across something called *The Writers' and Artists' Year Book*, my wife Bridget sat on the floor of the library laboriously copying out names and addresses of publishers and magazines that might be interested in my stuff. She sent out lots and lots of my bits and pieces, but the response was not very positive. One prominent editor was certain that his readers 'would not wish to see our Lord Jesus Christ represented in this way'. I cannot remember what Bridget had sent him to provoke this reaction, but I still have his letter. I might frame it one day.

There were a couple of encouraging moments. Edward England, something of a legend in Christian publishing, was kind enough to read some of my stuff, and wrote to say that he was sure I could write, but that I would need to find a great subject. True, of course, in any genre, but especially perhaps in the neurotically positive world of evangelical Christian literature.

Another very energising experience occurred when a letter arrived one morning from America. Bridget and I had been involved in a late-night television programme called *Join the Company*, broadcast each night in the south of England. Some months previously Bridget had met John and Elizabeth Sherrill in the course of recording one of these late-night discussions. The Sherrills were a hugely successful American husband and wife writing team, producing such iconic and universally best-selling titles as *The Cross and the Switchblade*. Elizabeth encouraged the other three programme participants to send her examples of their writing if they wished. Remembering this warmly expressed invitation, Bridget posted her a copy of *The Visit*, a short story I had written about Jesus arriving at a High Street church in the eighties.

The letter I received that morning brought tears to my eyes. Elizabeth wrote to say that, in all her years of reading works by new writers, she had never come across such potential quality. The gist of that wonderful communication was that, whatever I had been, or was now, or might be in the future, I simply *was* a writer. Something to do with identity. Those who have arrived at a point in their lives where they feel nakedly vulnerable in all circumstances will appreciate what it means to be handed such a warm and enveloping cloak when it is least expected and has certainly not yet been earned.

Elizabeth's letter was a powerful incentive to carry on with my scribbling, and opportunities for work were beginning to arise. After two or three articles had appeared in *Family Magazine* I was commissioned by a small Christian publisher to write a book about my own life and my encounters with guests and fellow-participants on *Join the Company*.

In retrospect it seems extraordinary that anyone, including me, believed it made sense to write an autobiography. The only people who would have heard of me were that tiny number of viewers in the south of England who, in the days before all-night television, stayed up to watch the very last programme of the day. Our viewers tended to be insomniacs, taxi-drivers, publicans and various groups of students who seemed to find our discussions hilariously funny. Considering the fact that we attempted to deal with such vast subjects as sex, death, terminal illness and the nature of God in less than ten minutes each, those students were probably right.

I wrote the book. Of course I wrote the book. Why would I not? It was called *Join the Company*, and Bridget and I were deeply, passionately thrilled when we were able to hold copies in our hands for the first time. I used to put it on the coffee table in our sitting-room, walk out, and then stroll casually back in and notice *my book* with a little shock of pleasure and surprise. Bridget did her own bit of casual strolling through our local Christian bookshop, surreptitiously turning round a copy that was tucked away on a shelf with only its spine showing, so that potential purchasers could see the front cover.

Join the Company was actually a lumpy, rather strange piece of work, but there was a sort of raw honesty about it. In those days Christian books usually offered spiritual techniques and solutions in one form or another. Lots of gloss. My book was a ragged tome, abounding in unre-solved issues and loose ends, but at least there was a stress-fuelled whiff of truth about it. Unsurprisingly, sales were not impressive. Later, after the *Sacred Diary* came out, *Join the Company* was republished as *The Growing Up Pains of Adrian Plass*, and was more successful.

The whole experience of writing a whole, real book was tough and very rewarding, but I had still not discovered that 'great idea' mentioned by Edward England. However, something else had already begun to happen.

The *Adrian Mole* books were hugely successful in the mid-eighties, and it was Andy Butcher, assistant editor of *Family Magazine*, who suggested that, given my Christian name, I might like to write a monthly humorous column for the magazine, to be entitled: 'The Secret Diary of Adrian Plass, aged 37 and three-quarters'.

That column was easy to put together. The fictional Adrian, a confused, earnest fellow, had a fictional wife called Anne (no, Bridget is not my second wife, as some people seem to think) and a sixteen-year-old son named Gerald, who became a vehicle for many of the points I so enjoyed making about silliness in the Church.

The ease with which ideas came was not so much because of my skills as a writer, but because I had found an unex-pected opportunity to transfigure life-stopping darkness into life-giving humour. It was a principle that was unfa-miliar to me, and I could certainly not have labelled it in that way at the time, but its execution was pure joy and satisfaction. So much dirty water flowing off my chest, and such an unbounded relief to hear myself laughing at the church-related problems and issues that I had been wearing like lead weights around my neck for years. Mind you, I thought I might be the only one who would laugh at my new approach to these 'serious' things. I soon learned that this was not the case.

A man who attended a local Evangelical Community Church (can there really be any other sort?) invited me to come along to a meeting of the youth group he was leading at the time. Colin had read a couple of my columns and thought the young folk might enjoy hearing them. I wasn't so sure. 'Young folk' tend not to filter their boredom as adults might. This is perfectly good and right for them, but dreadful for aspiring writers who are about to read out something that is supposed to be funny, but might not be. There is, after all, only one test for humour.

I went anyway. They laughed. They laughed a lot. It was a very satisfying evening and I took heart.

Colin, whose surname was Saunders, turned out to be significantly involved in the organisation of Spring Harvest, the big Christian family festival that, in those days, took place on several holiday camp sites around the country. Would I be interested, he wondered, in visiting one of these venues next April to entertain holidaymakers? Accommodation and food would be provided for myself and my family. We would just need to fund our travel.

Saying yes felt like an agreement to play golf in the dark. The whole thing was a mystery. A scary mystery. A wonderful opportunity to fail in front of huge numbers of people.

Three months later we took a coach to Prestatyn with our three children, our suitcases and our return fare plus a few pounds for emergencies and ice-creams. The journey seemed to take about six months, and we arrived wearily in Prestatyn with our three small children, only to find that we had arrived a day early, and would have to stay in one of those faded seaside Bed and Breakfast establishments where the walls are more thickly carpeted than the floors. Paying for this used up the money we had set aside for our return fare, but I suppose that is the nature of playing golf in the dark. We just had to get on with it and hope for the best. There was no other choice.

My first 'performance' at Prestatyn was a nightmare, at least to begin with. I found myself standing at a microphone in a huge holiday-camp venue, blinded by lights, with what seemed to be about an acre of dance floor separating me from hundreds of people back there in the dark who had no idea who I was. They were waiting for me to be funny. A muscle in my leg was throbbing so violently that I was sure it must be audible, my top lip was sticking to my teeth, and my mouth was as dry as the Gobi Desert. I croaked a few words. Nothing. I croaked a few more. Then the merest titter sparked from the darkness.

But it seemed to ignite the rest of the audience. Moments later the place was ablaze with laughter. The restorative effects of a positive response to humour are quite remarkable. Throbbing legs are stilled and strengthened. Top lips detach themselves from top teeth as dry mouths are magically lubricated. It was all quite amazing and wonderful. I had made people laugh with stuff that had come out of my troubled head! That was the long and short of it, and it felt very good indeed.

A bunch of teenage girls came over to speak to Bridget and me at the end of the evening.

'We were thinking,' said one of them to my wife, 'it must be a laugh living with him!'

'Oh, yes,' replied Bridget, possibly doing a quick mental flip back over events of the past couple of years. 'It's a real laugh living with him, all right. We get up in the morning and we have a laugh. Then we laugh over lunch and all through the afternoon and evening, and sometimes all through the night. Yes, you're right. It's just one big laugh . . .'

Other readings at Prestatyn were equally successful, but eventually our stay ended and we were forced to face the fact that we simply could not afford to pay for the journey home. I'm not sure what this says about us, but it never occurred to either Bridget or I to ask anyone at Spring Harvest for assistance with this problem. Perhaps it was just that financial helplessness can be a very hard habit to break.

It was as we wandered in a luggage-laden and rather bewildered fashion along the local High Street on the day of our theoretical departure that an unlikely solution suggested itself. One of us noticed an advertisement in a shop window. Vouchers for coach travel were being offered with every Mars Bar that was bought. We collected every silver and brown coin that we possessed, and found that we were able to raise just over four pounds. This enabled us to buy twenty Mars Bars and – wonder of wonders! – collect sufficient vouchers to cover all the fares for our coach trip. A real result, but you will not have failed to spot the down side. Only one item of food was available to the five of us in the course of that eternal journey. We all liked Mars Bars, we always had done, but our strictly limited diet did get a little depressing as the hours passed.

With the column in *Family Magazine* becoming increasingly popular, I was asked by my book publisher if I would be interested in expanding my columns into a book of the same name. Of course I would be interested. But how about making it 'Sacred' rather than 'Secret'? They agreed.

I wrote *The Sacred Diary* in an old caravan at the bottom of our garden, and Bridget sent off the handwritten sheets to the publisher. We had no idea at all of how it was likely to sell as a book. It was published in spring of the following year, and I was once more invited to Spring Harvest (Minehead this time) to perform extracts. On the day after my arrival it was suggested that I might like to come across to the bookshop area to sign copies of my new publication.

Nerves set in. No one would buy a book. Even if they did, they wouldn't want me to sign it. I trudged off to the signing with a heavy heart and kept my head down as I sat at the small table that buyers were supposed to approach to have their books signed. Ten minutes, I thought, and I'm out of here. Ten minutes of toe-curling embarrassment, and then it will all be over. Two of those minutes passed. A silence seemed to fall. Had everyone cleared off? I lifted my head.

Everyone seemed to be holding a copy of my book. I signed books for a couple of hours, and returned in a state of profound shock to the chalet where Bridget, the boys and our brand-new baby daughter were waiting to find out how it had gone.

How had it gone? Well, in terms of prospects for the future there had been nothing. Now, as if from nowhere there was something – and it looked as if it might grow.

It did grow. For Bridget and I the last two and a half decades of writing and speaking all over the world are evidence of that. For the last three years the two of us have been closely involved with the 'resurrection' of Scargill House, a conference and retreat centre in North Yorkshire, a place where we have learned, if we didn't know it before, that, in terms of genuinely helping others, laughter is definitely not the poor relation of serious ministry, whatever that is. Laughter and love, we are shown again and again, are essential to those who have been offered no adequate theology of devastation.

That understanding, a culmination and a confirmation of all that we have experienced over the last twenty-seven years, is probably the reason why this book is rather different from those early *Sacred Diary* publications. I am very far from being as unhappy as I was in those days, but the truth is that I find life, work, the Church and God much funnier and at the same time much more serious than ever before. Perhaps I have grown up a bit, and so, inevitably, has the Adrian of the *Diary*. We are the same people, but more so.

If there is a God, and it looks increasingly as though that may be the case, we have to face a couple of facts. One is that he is not looking for wonderful Christians, but for inadequate followers with a willingness to be obedient. Another is that the informal face of Christian living is and always was the true face of Jesus working in this world. That is why the Adrian in this book is able to deal, fearfully but faithfully, with the burden of a possible major tragedy in his life, while being utterly thwarted by the absurdly infuriating attentions of Minnie Stamp, a new *Diary* character who is determined to offer counselling and comfort to Adrian on every possible occasion, whether he needs it or not.

Darkness and light. Tears and laughter. Minnie Stamp and heroism. Tragedy and resurrection. Silliness and salvation. These are the wounds and the rewards of walking with Jesus, and they always will be.

I should add that, though my depiction of Scarleeswanvale is definitely not intended to be a portrait of Scargill House, some will undoubtedly recognise a few of the brushstrokes.

I do hope you enjoy reading this book as much as I have enjoyed writing it.

A question has just occurred to me, by the way. What if my name had *not* been Adrian?

Adrian Plass and the Church Weekend

I

Planning, Panic and Minnie Stamp

Have decided to resurrect my diary in order to keep a short journal recording highlights of the church weekend that Dennis has asked me to organise. Dennis Strang replaced dear Edwin Burlesford as chief elder of our church a couple of years ago, and he is a brilliant preacher and a very good man generally. I must say, though, that when he is not actually in action, as it were, he is one of the most extraordinarily laid back people I've ever met. In every situation, formal or informal, indoors or outdoors, regardless of the weather or the occasion or any presenting difficulties, he comes over like a man who is sunbathing in the Maldives. Our original conversation last year about organising this church weekend was a case in point.

DENNIS: (*apparently shielding his face from the sun with one hand and lazily rubbing sun cream onto his chest with the other, even though we are actually standing in the church porch with the rain pouring down outside*) Ah, Adrian, any chance of you and Anne organising a weekend away for the church next year some time?

ME: (*slightly taken aback*) Er, well, possibly – probably, yes. We've never had a proper one before, I don't think. Er, what sort of things would that involve, Dennis?

DENNIS: (*with just enough energy to speak before he tilts his Boycott trilby over his eyes and drops off to sleep with the sound of the seagulls wheeling and crying above his head*) Oh, nothing much. Choose a venue. Organise the programme. Come up with a theme. 'Where is the Love?' might be a good one. Contact everyone. Sort the money out. Check transport. That sort of thing. Just up your street, Adrian. OK? Zzzzzzz . . .

ME: (*quietly, so as not to wake him*) OK. Right then. Good. Right. We'll get on with that then.

Bit nervous about telling Anne. When I'd been home for a while I said, 'Oh, by the way, Dennis has asked me how I would feel about organising a weekend away for the church.'

Anne casually flicked over a page of her magazine and said, 'That's interesting. Well, there's no harm in his asking, is there? You can certainly give it some thought, can't you?'

Pause.

'Yes.'

'What?'

'Yes, I can give it some thought, especially as I've more or less said I'll do it.'

Anne put her magazine down.

'What does more or less mean? More? Or less?'

Started babbling.

'Well, a little bit more more than less perhaps. Less less than more. Actually, quite a long way along the less to more continuum.'

'What!'

'I suppose I may have inadvertently given the impression that er . . .'

Anne's deep intake of breath through her nose, and her signature 'mm!' noise through compressed lips has never boded well for me.

'What have you "inadvertently" done? You've told him you'll do it, haven't you?'

Pause.

'Haven't you, Adrian?'

'Well, Dennis did say that it was right up my street.'

Anne put her magazine down and looked at me for a moment without speaking.

'Darling, has Dennis ever *been* up your street? Has he ever had a good look round your street? Has he caught a glimpse of the unrescuable wreckage of projects that litter your street, my love? You have some fine qualities, sweetheart, but organising events is really not one of them.'

'It's not as bad as it sounds, because . . .'

Suddenly lost my nerve. When the 'darlings' and 'sweethearts' and 'loves' start flying around in such profusion it's time to take off the armour of God and put on something more substantial.

'Because what?'

'Er, because he actually asked if we'd both do it, and I said . . .'

'You said we would.'

'In a way, yes.'

'You said we would.'

'Sort of.'

'You said we would.'

'Almost.'

'You said we would.'

'Yes.'

Bit chilly after that. Anything I said about anything at all was diverted straight into the 'You've said we'll organise the church weekend' channel.

'Shall I put the telly on? It's your favourite programme about the department store.'

'Are you sure we've got time to watch the television? Shouldn't we be planning the church weekend that you've said we'll organise?'

'I'll take the rubbish out, shall I?'

'No, I'd better do it. You might meet some random person on the pavement who'll ask you to be in charge of something, and you'll agree, and then we'd have less time for organising the church weekend that you've said we'll be responsible for . . .'

Got a bit wearing after a while. Quite glad when bedtime came.

Came down in the morning to find Anne humming happily as she dropped bread into the toaster.

She said, 'Sorry I got so grumpy last night. Gerald's been on the phone.'

'Oh, yes.'

'Yes. I told him what Dennis suggested, and he said how about his church and ours getting together for a weekend away? They've already got somewhere booked and St Jim's will only have quite a small group. Lots of beds left apparently. Not always a good sign, of course.'

She glanced at a notepad on the shelf next to the toaster.

'Place called Scarleeswanvale Deep Peace Retreat Centre. It's in a village called Stanwick. Quite a bit further away than would be ideal, but I think we'd have trouble getting anywhere very local this close to the time. Gerald says this

Scarleeswanvale place is known to have had one or two problems in the recent past, but apparently they're offering really good discounts to churches to get the numbers up.'

Suddenly looked imploringly at me. Aaaah ... Such relief. When Anne looks imploringly at me it's like the sun bursting triumphantly from behind a cloud.

'Adrian, I'd love it! Gerald says Josey and Cameron are going. We'll all be together. And I'd be fascinated to see some of his people away from home. What do you think?'

Nodded solemnly and judiciously, trying to look as if this was a decision that would need some careful thought.

'Well, I'd have to check with Dennis, of course. Can't go off half-cocked with these things, you know, Anne. Got to keep people in the loop, if you see what I mean. Act responsibly, and all that.'

Anne said sweetly, 'Do you want your orange juice in a glass or over your head, darling?'

Rang Dennis that afternoon at his house and put the idea to him. Could have sworn I heard the sound of rippling waves lapping softly against a tropical shore in the background.

'Love it,' he said languidly, passing his glass across to the Cuban barman for another Pina Colada with a touch more rum and a little less pineapple. 'Sounds a great plan, Adrian. Go for it. Love to Anne.'

He rang off. Gone. Probably comfortably late for a barbecue of giant prawns and wild boar steaks down on the waterline.

Got quite excited after that. Anne really got into the whole thing, thank goodness. She always was very organised. Making lists all over the place and chatting animatedly to Josey and Gerald on the phone.

So glad Josey and Cameron, my sixteen-year-old grandson, are coming on the church weekend with Gerald. Cameron is a real box of tricks, if you know what I mean.

And Josey – Josey. I remember the first time we met our future daughter-in-law. Gerald and Josey had become close after being on the same course at Ridcliffe Hall Theological College in Camford. Anne and I were to meet her and Gerald in a restaurant in Barton Road near the college on a Friday evening, and I was ridiculously nervous. What would she make of me? What had she heard about me from my son? We met in the lobby of the restaurant. She turned out to be quite small and very pretty with short dark hair and the steadiest, kindest blue eyes I've ever seen.

She whispered, 'Are you as nervous as I am?'

'Terrified,' I replied.

She tucked her arm in mine and reached up on the tips of her toes to kiss me on the cheek. She's been doing that ever since. Anne and I fell in love with her that day, and we never fell out again.

Funny about love. You think you know something about it, but you only ever know a very small bit about a little piece of it. You think you know the different kinds of love. Being a son, a brother, a husband, a father, a friend – but there are always surprises. Josey was one. She found a place in me where no one else was living, and moved in.

Must be something wrong with me. I remember trying to talk to my friend Richard about this when Anne and I were on holiday near Middleton-in-Teesdale with the Cooks, shortly after Gerald and Josey had announced their engagement. Richard and I were walking down the footpath to High Force Waterfall after that part of County Durham had endured a fortnight of heavy rain. I said whimsically, and obviously not loudly enough, 'Do you ever think about all the different kinds of love, Richard?'

'Yes,' he replied emphatically, raising his voice against the increasing roar of the falls, 'as a matter of fact I do. I think I can still name quite a few. I used to study them as a sort of hobby.'

'What?'

'Do you want to hear some of the ones I know?''

Richard Cook? Different kinds of love? Study? Really intrigued. You think you know a man . . .

'Yes, all right, go on then.'

'Do you want them in alphabetical order? That's how I learned them.'

'Er, yes, I suppose so, if you like.'

'African collared dove, African mourning dove, Bar-shouldered Copper Neck Dove, Beautiful Fruit Dove, Black-naped Fruit Dove . . .'

Shouted like a maniac against the wind and water.

'*LOVES*, NOT *DOVES*, RICHARD!'

Richard was striding on into the spray, loudly and mechanically listing doves as he went.

'Jobi Dove, Key West Quail-Dove, Laughing Dove . . .'

'LOVES! LOVES!'

'Luzon Bleeding Heart Dove, Mountain Witch Dove, Red Turtle Dove, Tambourine Dove . . .'

Gave up. I seemed to have entered another, quite different

parallel universe. At the very least, standing under an unstoppable outpouring of water listening to an unstoppable alphabetical outpouring of every species of dove on the planet for no good reason has to be one of my slightly more unusual experiences.

Rather less pleased to have a call from Minnie Stamp one evening, informing me that she is definitely coming on the weekend.

Minnie is a junior school teacher who joined our church a few months ago. She's in her mid-thirties, thin rather than slim, with a head, body and legs that never seem to end up in a straight line, probably because she's always curling some part of herself in unsolicited sympathy. I know you're not supposed to notice these things, but she has a slight problem with pronouncing the letter 'r', especially, to my fevered imagination, when she says my name. Quite pretty in a soppy, daisy-chain sort of way, but really annoys me, mainly because she reacts to anything I say as though I've come to her for counselling.

One day in church last year, for instance, I asked her if she had anything to contribute to the Harvest Festival entertainment that I was quite happily organising. She tilted her head to one side and crinkled her eyes in a caring, compassionate sort of way.

She said, 'Oh, Adrian, is no one wanting to do your little supper thing?'

'What? Er, yes, no, I mean, there isn't a problem, Minnie. Quite a lot of people have signed up, thanks. It's not really a supper *thing*, and it's not that little. It's not actually *my* supper thing. All I'm doing is . . .'

'It gives you an excuse to go round and speak to people, doesn't it, Adrian?'

What kind of demented pixies does the government allow her to teach, for goodness sake?

'Minnie, I don't need . . .'

'We *all* lovey-dove you, Adrian. God loves you through us. You do know that, don't you? There's no need to feel tiny and lost. You're what I call one of God's little sad elves, always working away really hard to make us notice you. Well, we *do* notice you, and we lovey-dovey-*dove* you!'

Moistened the tip of her forefinger with her tongue and touched my forehead playfully. If she knew how close this little sad elf came to altering the shape of her face with the nearest blunt instrument she would have been appalled. Asked Anne afterwards how I could feel such rage surging up in me about such a relatively trivial thing. Why on earth would I feel such a powerful need to justify myself to someone who inflicts her patently ridiculous insights on me every time we meet?

She said, 'Adrian, what I reckon is that, most of the time, what other people think about us is none of our business. Having said that, there is a bit of the little sad elf about you. I never noticed it before. I must ask Gerald what he thinks.'

Hmm.

After I'd said hello to Minnie on the phone on that particular evening she said, 'You sound all grumble-chops, Adrian. Would it make your grumble-chops day go all merry and bright if I said I was coming along to support you at the churchy thing? Because I *am*!'

Could hardly say, 'God, no! No, on the contrary, I wish

we had a special anti-bursary fund for paying people like you to stay away.'

Actually said, 'Oh, that's – that's great, Minnie, really good. I'll put you down on the list.' Added hopefully, 'You do really want to come, do you? Only I don't think we're going to have any trouble filling up the places, so if you're just . . .'

'Mister Adrian Plass es*quire*!' she interrupted with mock severity, 'Minnie says you are to march *straight* off to the bathroom and look at yourself in the mirror and say, "I am a fairy light on God's Christmas tree, and everyone loves my twinkle." Promise you'll do that?'

'Well, I . . .'

'Promise?'

'Oh, all right . . .'

As I came out of the bathroom and got into bed that night, I said to Anne, 'Anne, do you love my twinkle?'

Silence for a moment.

'Not your very best feature, my darling,' she said.

Huh! Thought so.

I must say, having to organise one of these events makes you realise that an awful lot of folk in the church see life as a matter of making sure that they move as serenely as possible from one comfort zone to another. People who have always seemed quite relaxed and co-operative in the past suddenly develop all sorts of awkward corners and sharp edges that have to be smoothed and sanded down, as it were, by people like me, who never really knew what they were doing in the first place. The list of comments and questions and complaints makes interesting reading, especially when I add the responses that I would like to have made if I wasn't a Christian and married to someone who edits my life.

'Which way will the bed face in my room? I can't sleep if my feet are pointing towards the north or east. I should add that I also can't sleep if my head is pointing towards the south or west. However, I can sleep if my feet are pointing south or west, or if my head is pointing towards north or east.'
Yes, don't worry. All the beds at Scarleeswanvale are attached to Lazy Susan-style revolving discs so that they can be pointed and locked into your favoured direction.

'Are dream-catchers allowed? I empty the nightmares out of my dream-catcher into the bin each morning, ready for the next night.'
Ah, yes, of course, I'd forgotten that Jesus said to his followers, 'Take neither purse nor scrip nor shoes, but, whatever you do, don't forget your dream-catchers. They are, after all, the ultimate source of peace, and certainly not a load of horse-shit.'

'Will Eileen Jessop be there? We've hardly spoken since she mocked my special pavlova at the church Christmas party in 2011, and I can't see that changing any time in the near future.'
Yes, your dear sister in Christ, Eileen, will be there, ready and willing to be forgiven by you, a Christian who has been commanded to love and forgive your enemies. Good news, eh?

'I didn't realise the church weekend away would involve staying somewhere else.'
Sorry, my mistake. I suppose it was the word 'away' that caused the problem, was it? I can see how baffling that must have been. Inexplicably, everyone else understood perfectly.

We won't be expected to actually do anything, will we?
Good gracious no. Of course not. We shall all stay quietly and safely in our rooms for the entire weekend until it's safe to go home.

People changing their minds has been another problem.
'I'm sorry, I forgot about a previous arrangement.'
'We discovered we can't afford it and we never accept charity.'
'I must have got it wrong. I thought it was a different weekend/month/year/decade.'
'I'm having doubts and don't want to spoil it for others.'
'Sorry, but we've just come across a new, more vibrant church where our needs are better catered for.'
'Well, you see, it never occurred to me that it would involve missing *Casualty*.'
Honestly!

That's why it was so refreshing to get a phone call from William Ebson one day about coming on the church weekend. He and his wife Lorna are new additions to our church. He has a long, tapering nose that turns slightly to the left as you look at it directly from the front, and she has an even longer nose that turns at a very similar angle to the right.

They seem quite a lively couple (wanted to make sure that there were *double* bedrooms available at the Retreat Centre!), so I suppose this off-centre facial phenomenon could be the result of frequent passionate nasal contact over the years. Hard to say. Anyway, it was really good after so much messing about to hear someone state so definitely that they would be coming on our church weekend.

'Excellent!' I said to Anne. 'After all the shilly-shallying I've had to put up with it's such a relief to hear this kind of straightforward decision-making. Makes our job seem so much easier.'

'Is that the couple with the noses you're talking about?' asked Anne.

'That's right. Why?'

'Bit volatile, sweetheart. Anything could happen.'

Disagreed. Should have known better.

Recorded each subsequent phone call as it came.

Phone call from Lorna Ebson to say that, regrettably, she and her husband William have decided to separate, so they won't be coming on the weekend. Very sad, and unexpected, but these things do happen. Crossed them off my list.

Phone call from William Ebson to say that, after much prayer, he is certain in his spirit that, by the Grace of God, he and Lorna are getting back together and that they will therefore be coming on the weekend after all, if it's still all right. Great news! Put the Ebsons back on my list.

Phone call from Lorna Ebson to say that William and God may think they're back together, but she doesn't, and could

I take them off my list or allocate William a single room if he insists on coming alone? Took them off my list as a couple and pencilled in a single room for William.

Phone call from William Ebson confirming that he will be needing a single room at the church weekend. Inked him in.

Phone call from Lorna Ebson to say that she and William have just met and prayed together, and there was a mighty miracle of reconciliation. They won't now be separating, and they will, as requested previously, need a double room at the church weekend. Put them both back on my list. Tippexed William's single room out.

I have now written the word 'Ebson' so often that it's become meaningless. Interestingly, I did the same once with the word 'corduroy'. Got into my head like a bee trapped in a box.

'Corduroy, corduroy, corduroy, corduroy, corduroy, corduroy . . .'

Nearly drove me mad.

Saw Gerald and said in passing, 'I've been saying the word "corduroy" over and over in my mind this week.'

'Why?'

'Er, that doesn't matter. What I was going to say was that I've said it so many times that I can hardly remember what it means.'

He said, 'Come off it, Dad! You're not likely to forget that one, are you? As you well know, it's a type of road made of tree trunks laid across a hexagonal.'

Too taken aback to argue. Grabbed my Concise Oxford as soon as I could and checked it out. How does he *know* these things? Next morning as I was getting dressed Anne said, 'You haven't worn your tree trunk trousers for a long time, darling. I've laid them out across the hexagonal for you . . .'

These days it's hard to know if it's telepathy or texting.

In the end, gave up wondering if the Ebsons would make it. We've booked them in and are hoping for the best. Can't help wondering if they were originally drawn together by their common nose-docking issues.

Just to add to my troubles, at the end of a church meeting one evening Dennis removed his snorkel for long enough to say that he'd been thinking it would be very helpful to hold a plenary session towards the end of the weekend away, and would I like to lead it?

Said, 'Heh, yes, good thinking! I'd be more than happy to do that. In fact, I've always particularly enjoyed them – plenary sessions, I mean. The old – plenary sessions. Yeah, great!'

Wished, as he drifted dreamily away, perhaps for a scuba dive to enjoy the rainbow hues of tropical fish and natural coral, that I'd said straight away I don't know what a plenary session is. Why do I still do this? Why, in my mid-sixties, am I still defensively pretending I know things when I don't? What is a plenary session? Not the foggiest. Sounds sort of flat and beseeching. Must look it up when I get a moment. Thank Gog for Goodle.

Gerald came over one Saturday to talk over plans for the church weekend. Showed him a book I've just bought called

Creating a Spiritual Ethos by someone called Denver Mountainberger, who is, I believe, an American.

Gerald glanced at it and said, 'Hmm, odd, isn't it? Yet another number one, international bestseller. How come every American Christian paperback I've ever seen is a number one international bestseller? They can't all be, can they? I mean, by definition, surely *some* books have got to *not* be number one international bestsellers so that the other ones can be?'

Gerald always did enjoy exploring side-turnings more than chugging peacefully along the main road.

In one chapter, entitled 'A Very Special Time', Mountainberger describes how, during a weekend away, members of his church conducted one of their meals in silence, apart from the playing of inspiring and godly music at the end of the dining room. The result, he says, was a 'deepening of bonds with each other and with God, a truly heart-warming time, filled with love, grace and spiritual harmony through the eloquent though soundless meeting of our eyes.'

Thought we might have a shot at this during the weekend away. Read that little section to Anne in bed that night. She yawned and frowned and said, 'How do you *deepen* bonds? Don't you strengthen them or reinforce them or something? The bit you read sounds as if they're going to get imbedded in your flesh.'

Kept my temper. I said, 'Never mind all that. What do you think of the general idea of a silent meal?'

She yawned again, 'Ooh, I dunno . . . Thing is, it's a family weekend, right? What about the children?'

I said, 'Well, quite honestly, if parents can't control their children for one hour in a whole weekend there's something very wrong with the whole – with parents who can't do that. Anyway, don't you like the idea of a truly heart-warming time, filled with love, grace and spiritual harmony?'

Anne said, 'Oh yes, sounds wonderful. That's why I think a silent meal is probably a bad idea on a family weekend.'

Asked Gerald what he thought about my silent meal idea the next morning. I said, 'Mum doesn't seem very keen, but she doesn't always get things right. For instance, there was a time earlier this year when she thought she was wrong about something, but it turned out she was mistaken. So there you are. She's not always right.'

Went off to the toilet before he could say anything. Glanced back and saw him looking at me with a sort of wonder in his eyes. Nice to know you can impress your own son after all these years.

Before Gerald left for home after lunchtime I said as nonchalantly as possible, 'Do you go in for plenary sessions much at your church Gerald, or – or not?'

'Well – I suppose we do sometimes, yes. Why do you ask?'

'Oh, I was just wondering, you know, what sort of interesting things have happened at the ones you've run, or organised or – done?'

He looked at me after glancing at Anne, who was filling the dishwasher.

'Well, apart from anything else, it does depend on getting the temperature of the water just right, Dad. Don't you agree, Mum?'

'Oh, yes, got to get that right.'

'The temperature of the water?'

'Yes,' continued Gerald, 'I mean, if you're reckoning to personally wash every single person's feet really thoroughly you've got to make sure the water's not too warm and not too cold, and that it stays OK all through the washing. Got to make sure to have towels on hand as well, of course. Get all that right and anything can happen.'

'Right. Right. Right . . .'

Horrified! Washing everyone's feet? Every single person's feet? Really thoroughly? Given the choice I think I would prefer to be locked in and made to watch every episode of *EastEnders* that's ever been made until I know the scripts by heart.

Heard Anne and Gerald laughing together in the porch a few minutes later as they said goodbye. When Anne came back I asked what was so funny.

She said, 'Oh, nothing darling. Nothing important. Honestly.'

Hmm.

Very frustrating news this morning, just days short of our weekend away. Alf Sanderson is an old friend of ours and one of the wardens at St Peter's, the church in Cawfield that is due to be supplying our speaker and our children's workers for the church weekend.

Alf phoned to say that the St Peter's community has suffered some sort of implosion. Not very surprised really.

Immediately obvious that James Galston, their vicar, who
arrived a few months ago, is facing an apparently inevitable
'Anglican Spring' – not unlike an Arab Spring, but minia-
ture and peculiarly Anglican in nature. My son, who trained
with James, characterises him as one of those people who
are quite happy to discuss the theology of love as they
strangle rabbits, and would probably deal with congregation members in a similar way if they could find a loophole
in canon law that allows it.

Gerald visited James at his previous church and told how,
as he walked through the main door, he came across him in
a one-sided discourse with what Gerald described as 'one
of those very white, puffy girls who tend to use their vicars
as emotional receptacles'. On seeing Gerald, Galston more
or less threw the poor girl away. Lucky not to be strangled,
Gerald said. She went spinning across the aisle, bounced
off the end of a pew, and, after dusting herself down a bit,
stood waiting, bruised and bovinely patient, for her chosen
receptacle to be free once more.

We knew there had been growing conflict between the
vicar and the good folk of St Peter's, particularly since the
occasion when he decreed that members of the youth group
must sign a declaration of faith before singing carols at the
shopping centre. We didn't realise it was about to come to
such a head.

'I'm afraid,' said Alf glumly, 'it was the business of your
weekend that sparked it all off in the end. Reverend Galston
says he wasn't told that David and the two ladies were
coming up to lead your groups. He got very hot under the
collar and sent messages out all over the place criticising
people for making decisions without consulting him when

he was supposed to be the one in charge. Well, you don't say that to people in your church, do you? I did try to suggest it might not be the best road to go down, but there we are. After that people started spraying e-mails around like a bunch of firemen let loose with high-pressure hoses, and the vicar ended up trying to lay the law down. He told David and June and Valerie point blank that they weren't allowed to come to you. Then everything blew up big-time, of course, and it's all come to a head, so this coming weekend there's going to be a big punch-up of a church meeting . . .'

'So, either way, David and the others need to be there.'

'Really sorry, Adrian.'

'Not your fault, Alf. Really hope the meeting goes OK. God bless.'

What a great team they would have been. Disaster! Have to think again.

Good news about speakers for our weekend away – I hope. I phoned Scarleeswanvale yesterday to tell them our theme and ask if they knew of any local people who might be available for our weekend. Got an e-mail this morning from the warden, a man called Alan Varney. Written rather in the style of those old-fashioned telegrams where you had to be as brief and staccato as possible because you were charged by the word.

'Mr Plass. Office enquired locally. Found speaker for two Saturday morning sessions only. Stanley Blorgan. Two children's workers. Megan Stride and Sarah Pile. Can't vouch but are available. Yes or no? Varney.'

Read it out to Gerald on the phone.

He said, 'Hmm, chatty little note, isn't it? Such a

seductively poetic tone. Not much choice really, though, is there, Dad? We don't want our own people to miss everything else by having to do it, and losers can't be choosers, or whatever the saying is. Let's go for it.'

Told Anne. She said, 'Blorgan, Stride and Pile, eh? Sounds like one of those evil Dickensian law firms. Still, I expect it'll be all right.'

Hope so.

Tried to ring Dennis, but he was out. I left my message after a 'speak' tone that sounded eerily like a note played on the top string of a Hawaiian guitar . . .

Ah well, trust God and keep your gun oiled, as my grandfather used to say.

One very good piece of news. Father John, who is a monk in an increasingly small order in Scarborough, and an old friend of Edwin's, is coming on the weekend. *So* pleased! A wonderful mixture of refreshing ordinariness and whimsical mysticism, this man has been a bit of a beacon to Anne and me over the years. His God seems much nicer and a lot wittier than the one most of us think we know. Dropped him a line on the off-chance, asking if he could make it, and he sent me a lovely note.

Dear Adrian
I am getting ridiculously old. Hope continues to swell in me like a balloon, while my body shrinks like something that has been washed on the wrong setting. I keep telling people that the next thing I do will be the last thing I do, but it never is – not so far, anyway. Yes, I would love to come to your weekend. I know that dear

Edwin will not be there. He has done his last thing in this world, and pioneered off to find out if all the things we claim to believe are true. You may be interested to hear that I am still in touch with Victoria and Stenneth Flushpool, and even more regularly with lovely Young Andromeda, who is, of course, no longer young except in comparison with me. She is even more lovely, though, and considerably more useful to God now that her wonderfully combative nature is under his control. I suspect that those old friends are unlikely to be with you, but I would be so happy to see you and lovely Anne and Gerald and Josey once more. Cameron must be quite grown up by now. A second Gerald? Beware, Church! Beware, world!

Of course, I was deeply reluctant to go against the divine will, so, inspired by something you wrote many years ago, I sought guidance. I humbly suggested to God that if General Booth, driving a purple Rolls Royce and singing 'The Laughing Policeman', drew up outside our front door at 11:36 this morning, I would know he was not keen on the idea. I have been watching through the window with bated breath since 11:35, but it is now 11:38, and as the great general never suffered from porphyrophobia and was invariably punctual, I am delighted to write this letter. See you soon!

Lots of love to all,
Father John

Time passes so quickly. Tomorrow we set off for Scarleeswanvale. Can't believe it! Do hope it goes OK. I used to be optimistic about everything God asked me to do. Then I went through a phase of thinking everything was bound to go wrong because it so often did. Now I know that things are rarely as good as I think they're going to be, and almost never as bad as I worry they're going to turn out.

Showed Anne this paragraph just now, and asked if she thought it indicated a growth in maturity.

She said, 'Yes, darling, you've very nearly caught up at last. Well done.'

Is that a compliment?

Anyway, from tomorrow I shall try to keep an hour-by-hour record of things that seem important during the weekend. Might be a useful template for those who organise similar events in the future.

2

Friday Morning

Up in good time. Very exciting!

Rang Leonard Thynn early this morning to check that he and his wife Angels know where the conference centre is and how to get there. Never forgotten a trip with Leonard some years ago when I was driving and he was (in theory) in charge of the map. He managed to spot each turn and change of direction OK, but usually just after we should have turned or changed. After about an hour of being infuriated by this maddening, retrospective navigation I stopped the car in a lay-by and asked why on earth he couldn't tell me what I needed to do before I needed to do it.

'I didn't want to distract you, Adrian,' said Thynn. 'The last thing you want is someone talking to you just as you're about to turn off or pull out into a main road or something like that.'

'Yes, but, Leonard, don't you see that if you don't tell me when to turn or which way to go I can't do it, so distracting me isn't an issue. It doesn't come into it, does it? There's nothing to be distracted from, is there?'

'Ah, yes, but when you have to go further up the road and find somewhere to turn round and come back to the place where you should have turned off in the first place, it gives you lots of time to think about it and make sure you get it right, doesn't it? So, in a way, I *am* telling you well in advance, aren't I?'

Not for the first time I just sat and stared at Thynn, wearily conscious that using my brain to communicate with his was about as pointless as using an Inuit phrase-book to enquire about buses in Azerbaijan.

All I wanted to know on this particular morning was that Leonard and Angels would be able to get there in time for the evening meal.

'Ah,' said Leonard, 'we know we'll be fine because we've bought one of those things that you stick to your wind-screen and wait for someone to tell you how to get where you want to go.'

'A Satellite Navigation System, you mean?'

Pause.

'No, it's one of those things that you stick to your wind-screen and . . .'

'That's what a Satellite Navigation System is, Leonard. A SatNav, people call it. Are you sure you're going to be able to use it?'

'Yes, Adrian, Angels and I have studied the instructions very, very carefully. They're amazing things, aren't they?'

'Yes, they are. Well, I'm glad you and Angels have – you know, taken the time to work out how to use the one you've got.'

'Thank you, yes. By the way, one little point. We've been wondering how the little person in the Sad Nav thing knows where you want to go in the first place. Who tells them?'

Silly me. Of course it was too good to be true.

'Leonard, there isn't a little person in the Sad Nav – I mean the SatNav. You have to enter the information that I've sent you and let the person who . . .'

'So there is a person. Why did you say there wasn't – oh, hold on, Adrian, Angels is calling me. I'll have to go. See you at the conference centre this afternoon. Bye!'

Oh dear.

Suddenly remembered as we were setting off for Stanwick that I still hadn't worked out what a plenary session is. Don't really want to ask Anne. Wished I hadn't left it so late.

3

Friday Afternoon

Arrived at Scarleeswanvale Deep Peace Retreat Centre around 2.30 p.m. Not a lot of deep peace about. Frenzied atmosphere in the Reception Office, with two frantic, wild-eyed young women huddled over lists and badges and forms. Atmosphere reminded me of the bit in *Titanic* – just after hitting the iceberg, when they're poring over plans of the ship and realising that everyone's going to die.

Gave them our names and waited while they studied their charts and stuff, and knocked badges on the floor and almost swore and picked them up again.

One of them, chewing a pencil ferociously, looked up and said with a nervous but hopeful expression on her face, 'So, you'll be the Huddersfield bryologists, won't you?'

Short silence.

'Er, no,' said Anne, 'we won't.'

'Are you *sure*?' Looked down at her list again for a moment. 'No, look I'm sorry, but I don't see how you can't be. You *must* be!'

'Well, I'm sorry too, but we can't be because – well, primarily because we're not,' replied Anne patiently.

'Not the Huddersfield ones?'

'No, not even the Huddersfield ones. In fact, I don't even know what a bryologist is. Do you know what a bryologist is, Adrian?'

Shook my head.

'A bryologist is someone who studies *moss*,' said the girl, throwing her hands out and emphasising the last word of her sentence. She stared with a sort of slightly annoyed but pleading expectancy at Anne, as though this crucial piece of information might jog her into remembering that she was a bryologist living in Huddersfield after all, and then everything would fall into place and get sorted out.

Anne said, 'No, no, as I've already said, our names are Adrian and Anne Plass, we have only the tiniest, *tiniest*, most miniscule interest in moss, and we're part of the organising team for the joint churches weekend away. My husband and I have definitely been booked in for quite a while.'

More tense hissing and whispering and sighing accompanied by frantic pushing back of hair and chart studying.

'Right! Right! I think we've sorted it out. It'll be fine. It'll be fine! It *will* be fine! Right! Mrs Plass, you've got a top bunk in the annexe down in the village at the bottom of the hill, so that's handy for supervising your schizophrenic recovery group, and Mr Plass will be here in the main building in what we call the 'Little Pod' right up at the top of the tower, with its own trapdoor and everything. I'll just give you your badges and . . .'

'Sorry, sorry, sorry, can I just stop you there.'

Noticed Anne's politeness had become a tad icy.

'I know this is a difficult job and you're working very hard, but I need to tell you two things – no, three things. First, I am not going to sleep in a bunk in the annexe down in the village. Secondly, we do not have a schizophrenic recovery group in our church and, however sympathetic I may feel towards the person who *is* supervising the one that appears to be gathering in the annexe, and believe me I do feel sympathetic with them and with their group, it is not going to be me. Thirdly, my husband is not going to sleep like Rapunzel in any "little pod" right up at the top of the tower. We are going to sleep together – *go* to sleep together, that is – in the en-suite room – *en-suite* room – in the main building. The room that we booked some time ago. That is what we are going to do.'

Brief, churning silence. Followed by much stormy sighing.

'Actually, there is a vacant en-suite room,' piped up the one who hadn't spoken yet, excitedly prodding a little box on the chart with her finger, 'as long as you don't mind sharing a bathroom and toilet.'

Was about to say that would be fine, but Anne said, in the sort of tone you might use with a recalcitrant schizo-phrenic recovery group member, 'Ah, but we do mind, don't we, because, you see, sharing a bathroom and toilet would fall significantly short of the commonly accepted defini-tion of an en-suite bedroom, wouldn't it?'

'Just a minute, just a minute, I think I've got it!' said the first one to her colleague. 'Look, Janice, we could put twenty-four and thirty-two into fifteen, then tell forty-nine (that's Sally, and she never minds moving) she has to share with thirty-six just until the day after tomorrow when twenty-eight goes and we can move them into twelve, and then forty-nine can go into twenty-eight leaving thirty-two with fifteen and giving twenty-four the choice of going back to twenty-four or changing to thirty-six or fifty-nine because they're both moving into seventeen on Sunday anyway. If we do all that, we can put Mr and Mrs Plass into thirty-seven, which is an en-suite. The only thing is . . .'

Anne said suspiciously, 'Ye-e-e-s, tell us about the only thing.' She laughed lightly, as though at an absurdity. 'You're not going to ask us to change our names, are you?'

Short, difficult silence.

'Er, well, I know it might sound a bit silly, but how *would* you feel about changing your names to Mr and Mrs Dabeney – just while you're here for the weekend, of course?'

'Oh, not for the rest of our lives, then? You had me worried there for a minute.'

Nervous laugh.

'No, it's just that it would save us an awful lot of extra work here in admin. The badges are all done and everything . . .'

So lovely to see Gerald, Josey and Cameron when they turned up soon after that. Gerald and Cameron much as usual. Like matching Babushka dolls in terms of looks and humour. Josey as sweet as ever, but she gave my arm an extra hard squeeze when she kissed me, almost as though she was sharing a secret. Strange. Vaguely worrying.

Told Anne that I quite fancied the idea of settling down with the mysterious Mrs Dabeney for the night.

She said, 'Forget it, Rapunzel, or I shall get you podded.'

The written names on our hastily prepared badges are very difficult to read. We'll have to get them sorted later. I appear to be someone called 'EDRAIN BASS'. My wife seems to be 'ANDA PULSE'. Gerald says I sound like an Amish backslider who's gone away for a dirty weekend with a Scandinavian porn star. Not a relationship made in heaven – or anywhere else, for that matter.

People from both churches flooded in as the afternoon went on. Faces known and unknown, and kids running around all over the place. Predictable mix of uncertainty and heartiness. Neither of these applied to a tall, angular, rather shockingly intense looking man with a laterally mobile jaw, presumably from Gerald's church, poking his head through the reception window and barking at the people in the office as I was bringing in someone else's bags. Seemed to be getting a bit irate.

'Well, do please forgive me for my failure to think ahead. I foolishly supposed that ten months might be sufficient notice of my arrival. If I had realised that I needed to book my place here shortly after I was born I would of course have insisted on my parents getting in touch with you immediately the midwife placed me into their care. Perhaps even that would have been too late, would it? If only my grandparents had had the common sense to contact you just after the war.

'Rumour has it that this is, theoretically, a Christian establishment. If that is the case, would it be asking too much for that theoretical Christianity to impinge on the way in which you actually operate, or am I being unreasonable?'

Ran into Gerald giving high fives to two little girls with ice-cream cone hair in the Moon Lounge. Told him what was happening and asked who the man was.

He groaned and said, 'Oh, goodness, I'd better go and rescue those poor people. Sounds like Alvin Dekkle, our

Fresh Expressions evangelist. He's been foisted on us – I mean, helpfully supplied to us – by the bishop, who couldn't find anywhere else to dump him – place him. Josey's very big on the Fresh Expressions thing, and she likes him like she likes everybody, but she does say he spends a lot of time sitting around looking as if the component elements of the very air itself are ganging up on him. He never helps with moving chairs or setting up for services, and he does seem to have a gift for falling out with all sorts of people. Remember that anagram of "evangelist" you put in one of your books, Dad? "Silage vent", wasn't it? Are you *sure* you haven't met Alvin before? Let me go and straighten things out.'

Gladys Merton, a very elderly, sweet-natured lady from our church beckoned me over to her seat in the Moon Lounge as I passed through on my way to the office. Gesturing for me to bend down close to her she whispered nervously in my ear.

'Adrian, I hate to make a fuss, and I'm quite embarrassed about putting people to extra trouble, but do you think it's going to be all right about my silly eating problems? I *think* I remembered to put it on my form. Do I need to speak to anyone else about it, or . . .?'

Took one of her hands in mine.

'Gladys, you're brilliant! You've reminded me that I'm supposed to give the kitchen a list of all our special dietary needs, including yours – there are a few, so you're not the only one. I'll go and do it right now. Thanks for your help.'

Left Gladys beaming in the Moon Lounge and fetched the list I needed from our bedroom. Large, smiley, middle-aged lady took the sheet of paper from me at the kitchen hatch and glanced at it briefly.

'Not too difficult for you I hope?'

She laughed.

'Not at all. No problem. We want people to enjoy their food. One or two of the young ones can be a bit insensitive about this sort of thing, but we're teaching 'em, bit by bit. Anyway, your list is nothing compared with some of the folk we get in. Mind you,' she continued, tapping a laminated sheet of paper Blu-tacked to the wall beside the hatch, 'none of them have ever been as bad as this. Before my time, so we're not sure if it's for real or not, but it gives us a laugh and reminds us that things could always be worse.'

She peeled it from the wall and handed it to me.

'Take it away and have a read. Might make you chuckle. Stick it back when you've finished. My name's Meg.'

'I'm Adrian. Thanks, Meg.'

Ebsons arrived at the reception area late-ish, with their mis-matched noses and their bags. Both looked stony-faced and grim. Lorna took Anne and me aside for a chat.

She said, 'Adrian, I'm so sorry to begin the weekend with bad news, but during our journey here William and I have decided that our marriage is finally and irrevocably over. We shall stay one night in our allocated room so as not to inconvenience anybody.'

No, well, they certainly wouldn't want to do that, would they? Inconvenience people? Who? The Ebsons? No-o-o-o.

'Then in the morning William will move to a single room if one is available, and I shall go home.'

Anne said gently, 'Lorna, are you really sure about this?'

Lorna said slowly and gravely, 'Anne, after tonight William and I will never sleep under the same roof again. Heaven and earth may, by God's grace, come together and be renewed and reunited in the fullness of time, but we shall not.'

Went up to sixty-three, the Ebsons' room, just before four o'clock to tell them tea was ready and I'd sorted out a single room for William tomorrow. Was about to knock when I realised there was a sound of bedsprings and heavy breathing coming from the other side of the door. Hoped they weren't fighting. When I knocked there was sudden silence, followed by what sounded like frantic rushing around and tidying. Door opened just a crack at last, and Lorna Ebson, bright-eyed and rather flushed in the face peered out at me.

'Ah, sorry to bother you, Lorna – just to say that tea's all ready and I've managed to find a single room for William for tomorrow, so . . .'

'Oh! Yes. Er, we wanted to talk to you about that. William and I feel that it may be worth having er . . .'

Tried to be helpful.

'One more go?'

'Er, yes, precisely. Yes. One more go. We shall er – we shall be down shortly, after er . . .'

'One more go?'

Pause.

'Er, that's right, yes.'

Closed the door carefully so as not to catch Lorna's nose and went back down to the conservatory.

Met a very nice lady on my way, wandering along the corridor laden with pillows and sheets and carrier bags and a duvet. Asked if I could help. She introduced herself as Sally, a regular volunteer at Scarleeswanvale.

I said, 'Ah, you must be the lady we heard about earlier who was going to move from forty-nine to share with thirty-six and eventually end up in – was it twenty-eight?'

'It was,' said Sally mournfully but resignedly, 'only that hasn't worked out because the office got the wrong week and all the room numbers were wrong. I don't really mind, but now I have to go into thirteen until fifty-one's free, and then everything depends on whether the man from the village comes to mend the bed in sixty-two. I feel a bit like one of those wandering Arabs who roam round the desert with their tents all the time. I don't really mind, but . . .'

Sympathised, and helped carry her stuff to the next oasis, but someone had just moved into thirteen, so Sally patiently dumped her stuff on the floor and went off to ask the people in the office where to go next. Hope she lands somewhere soon.

When I got back down Anne said, 'Well, how are the Ebsons doing?'

Whispered, 'I think there's been another miracle of reconciliation. Quite a lively one by the sound of it. They're having one more go. At least one. '

After tea, Josey arrived at my side, took my arm and asked if we could take a little time together after all the introductions this evening because there was something she wanted to tell me.

Spent quite a bit of the next hour or so wondering what she was going to say. Josey is one of my great gifts from

God. A pearl of great price. A real, real friend. The only daughter-in-law I'll ever have, and the way she seems to love me takes my breath away. It doesn't make sense. Like finding that someone's stuck a load of money in your bank account for no reason. There's always the fear that it was some kind of mistake and they'll want it back. You're lucky if you're given one person like Josey in your life. I've got four. I'm rich.

Asked myself the same thing over and over again as I sorted people out and carted luggage up and down stairs and tried to deal patiently with everyone's problems: What was Josey going to tell me?

Finally got a chance to sit down in the little morning room next to the Moon Lounge just as the five-minute warning bell started to clang ear-blastingly through the building, wielded with unrestrained relish by a young Community member who was clearly determined that no one was going to be late for dinner if he had anything to do with it. Picked up the list that Meg had lent me and took a moment to read it.

SPECIAL DIETARY REQUIREMENTS FOR GUEST IN ROOM 24, 17-25 SEPTEMBER 2007

- Fat free, wheat free, dairy free, sugar free, lactose free, gluten free.
- No meat or fish or eggs, of course.
- Nothing cooked in oil.
- Also no soya, pulses, legumes or nuts, or any food prepared in a kitchen where nuts or pulses or legumes or soya have been prepared.

- No processed food or anything containing artificial sweeteners, additives, colouring or flavourings, including salt, herbs and spices.
- No carbonated beverages. No fruit juices. No caffeine, tannin or cocoa.
- No tomatoes (high acid content), no cherries, apricots, peaches or plums (cyanogenic glycosides), no rhubarb (oxalic acid salts) or melons, bananas, dates or oranges, because of potassium. Please, no rice or pasta – even gluten free (high on the glycemic index), no potatoes (glycoalkaloids) or chocolate (alkaloid theobromine) and strictly no nutmeg (myristicine) or kidney beans (phytohaemagglutinim).
- No crops where pesticides, fertilisers or herbicides have been used in the last twenty years, and please, no fruit or vegetables that have been packaged, as there is always a danger of bacteria being added.

She says, 'Apart from the things on my list I love everything. In fact I have to confess that food is one of my little weaknesses.'

Smiled and waved at Meg, busy in the bowels of the kitchen, as I stuck her startling special needs list back on the wall. She smiled back, waved with one hand and wiped her brow with the other.

4

Friday Evening

Everyone except Leonard and Angels safely arrived by the time Gerald had said grace and we were all seated ready for dinner to be served. Lovely to see Father John in his scruffy old habit tied at the waist with a rope. Still smiling away and spreading peace and laughter like others share their colds. So frail, though.

Our replacement speakers have arrived as well. Stanley Blorgan looks OK. Tallish, heavily built with rather a lot of teeth, but very chatty and friendly. Earlier on after tea he had disappeared energetically into the Hexagonal Lounge, which is where we'll be meeting, laden down like a packhorse with books and piles of paper and bits of equipment. Seems very keen.

The children's workers are a different kettle of fish. Gerald commented worriedly that Megan Stride and Sarah Pile look like women who failed their audition for *The Addams Family* because they look too scary. The bigger one, Megan, has large, unblinking eyes in a dead-white oval face, and a halo of prematurely greying, lank hair. Sarah Pile has short jet-black hair that stands straight up from her head, and a permanent expression of shocked horror on her face, as though she once experienced a severe electric shock and has been trying to work out what happened ever since. Oh, dear. What will the children make of them?

*   *   *

Must say, the Community members do vary enormously. Most of the kitchen team couldn't be kinder or more caring towards guests when they serve them at mealtimes. By contrast, a stout, unsmiling young man serving dinner this evening seems to leave a lot to be desired. Appeared from the kitchen door holding a meal on a plate, and called out in a loud, passionless voice, 'Where's the gluten-free?'

Little Gladys Merton, who was sitting on Gerald's table, meekly identified herself as 'the gluten-free', but was clearly troubled by what she saw when the plate was plonked unceremoniously in front of her. She called out nervously to her 'waiter' who had already turned away to head for the kitchen.

'Er, excuse me, I'm awfully sorry to bother you, but I did say on my form that I was lactose-intolerant as well as needing to have gluten-free food. This looks lovely, and I'm very grateful, but I really can't eat some of these things, because if I do . . .'

Still completely without expression, the young man interrupted with a sound pitched somewhere between a sigh and a grunt, then bellowed in the direction of the kitchen.

'Can you check the list, see if the gluten-free on table four is lactose-intolerant as well?'

Gerald abruptly rose to his feet and called out in an almost exactly similar tone, 'And can someone check that the courtesy-free, decency-intolerant standing next to table four has officially been let loose on innocent guests.'

The young man looked furious, but as Gerald's interjection was greeted by a round of applause, he could only retreat with flaming cheeks. Minutes later a dark-haired girl with an Eastern European accent delivered the appropriate meal with a flashing smile and a heartfelt apology for lovely Gladys.

I felt so proud of my son.

Still no sign of Leonard and Angels by the time coffee was served in the Moon Lounge after dinner. Borrowed the office phone to ring Leonard on his mobile. Got through after about three goes. Usual bewildering headache of a conversation.

'Hello, Leonard, it's Adrian here. Just wondered how you and Angels were getting on.'

'Hello, yes, we're doing fine.'

'Good, which road are you on?'

'The M6.'

'The M6? But that's the wrong – which way on the M6? North or south?'

'Er, both.'

'Both? What do you mean – both?'

'We've been on the same little bit of the M6 for quite a long time, Adrian.'

'Why?'

'Erm, we're not very good at counting the exits off the roundabouts. Katy says . . .'

'Katy?'

'The lady in the SatNav thing keeps saying things like, "At the roundabout take the fifth exit," and we try to count them, but we keep counting roads that aren't exits and going down the wrong one. We went down one just now that wasn't an exit at all. It was the opposite of an exit. It was an entrance. That was quite dangerous. We both screamed when a lorry nearly crushed us. Then each time that happens we have to go back onto the M6 and try again. We've been up and down the same bit of the motorway ever so many times. Angels says it's like one of those strange films where you have to live the same little piece of your life over and over again, and she's getting a bit frightened.'

'But, Leonard, all you have to do is come off the exit that's signposted to Stanwick. You don't need to actually count the exits. Ignore the SatNav and just follow the signs.'

Pause.

'Katy will be cross.'

'Katy? Who's Katy?'

'I told you – the lady in the SatNav thing.'

'No! Leonard, she's just a . . .'

Phone went dead.

Just to make polite conversation before leaving the office, I asked the slightly severe lady who was guillotining sheets of A4 at the desk what she was working on.

She looked at her sheets of paper.

'Oh, these, you mean. In the past we always sent hand-written letters expressing love and support to former Community members when we heard that there were prob-lems in the part of the world where they lived. All sorts of natural disasters and crises, all over the world. Mr Varney has decided that we should use a less time-wasting, more efficient process. These are ready-printed letters that simply have to be deleted appropriately. They live in that tray over there marked "Compassionate Response".'

She held out one of her half A4 sheets.

'Have a look if you want.'
I took it.
'Thank you.'

PERSONAL LETTER OF SUPPPORT TO
OPPRESSED FRIENDS AND CONTACTS

Dear friend / companion / volunteer / former Community member / prospective Community member / ___ (delete or insert as appropriate), *this is just to assure you that we are thinking of you as you face the tsunami / earthquake / nuclear accident / civil unrest/ oppressive dictatorship / forest fire / hurricane / bird flu / ___* (delete or insert as appropriate) *that your homeland of Uganda / Australia / Libya / New Zealand / Japan / Pakistan / Isle of Wight / ___* (delete or insert as appropriate) *is suffering / has suffered / is about to suffer* (delete as appropriate). *Please believe, dear* (insert name), *that we think of you and pray for you occasionally / frequently / without a pause* (please select commitment), *and we hope to see you again in the immediate / near / distant / indeterminate* (indicate likelihood) *future.*

> *Yours with love and deep sincerity,*
> *The Scarleeswanvale Community*

Hmm. Not sure what to make of that.

Warden came to welcome us in the Hexagonal Lounge after tea and coffee while the children went off into their own group with Megan and Sarah, or 'The Dark Forces' as my grandson Cameron has already christened them.

Alan Varney turns out to be medium height and stocky with bushy eyebrows, piercing eyes, dark, straight, toilet-brush hair and an extraordinarily pointed head. He seems very angry and Welsh. Said he was going to give a brief reflection at the end of the welcome. (Not that there's anything fundamentally wrong with being Welsh, of course.)

Went through a list of housekeeping bits and pieces, then said he was happy to answer any questions.

Gerald asked if there was any likelihood that the fire alarm, if it sounded, would have any synchronistic parallel with the possibility of there being an actual fire. One or two people who seemed to appreciate the humour of this question laughed lightly. Alan Varney stared uncomprehendingly, and ignored Gerald completely.

There was a second query. Someone asked, 'How many staff do you have here at Scarleeswanvale?'

'None!' barked Varney. There was a slight tinge of triumph in his voice, as though he had captured the questioner in a strategically placed ambush. 'We are a Community, we are not an hotel.'

An hotel?

'Some of the people who work on our kitchen team, for instance, have never done that kind of work before. Please bear that in mind. The only requirement is that they do their very best.'

Dear old Richard Cook piped up.

'Winston Churchill said that doing our best is not enough, sometimes we have to do what is required.'

'Is that a question?'

Pretty rude.

'Sorry.' Poor Richard sounded rather deflated, 'I just wondered if you agree with him.'

'Personally I have little interest in the Gospel according to Saint Winston,' replied Varney drily. 'Crudely sculpted aphorisms from pugnacious alcoholics are no substitute for Scripture, in my view. Any further questions?'

'It's like having Jesus himself in the room, isn't it?' whispered Gerald.

'Excuse me, I have a question.'

It was an elegant, older lady who'd spoken.

'One of ours,' murmured Gerald with a little anticipatory smile on his face. 'Should be interesting.'

'I was just wondering,' said the questioner in slightly hoarse, but beautifully modulated tones, 'given the scope and responsibility of the job that you do here, how you manage to remain so delightfully warm and gracious in your dealings with people like us, who are bound to disrupt the smooth running of Community life.'

Varney glared suspiciously at the speaker, but when I turned round to look there was nothing but polite enquiry on the long, horsey face.

'The Community exists for the benefit of the guests,' he said shortly. 'Indeed, guests are marginally easier to deal with, because they do, at least, go home eventually.'

This unexpected excursion into Varney's very own sledgehammer style of humour was greeted with one or two nervous titters, but *Sunday Night at the Apollo* this was not.

'I mentioned', continued Varney, 'that we operate in teams here. Normally I would briefly explain the function of these teams, but Alison Bates, our *creative* director' – he pronounced the word 'creative' rather as though it was a sexually transmitted disease – 'has written a presentation in rhyming verse which she and some of the Community members would now like to perform. I have not seen or heard it myself,' he added rather unnecessarily.

Alison Bates, a fresh and delightful looking lady in her thirties dressed in tracksuit and trainers, ran briskly out to the front with four other younger people and arranged the group in a row facing us. Alison smiled brightly.

'Evening! Hello everybody! Lovely to have you here.'

General sigh of relief throughout the room. A human being!

'Right, we're going to do our little poem to give you a bit of an idea about the teams and the people who work here at Scarleeswanvale. There are ten verses altogether, so we're doing two each. Some of the names you'll hear: lovely Jane is the lady who's in charge of Finance. Bit scary sometimes, but the whole place would fall apart without her. Steve's our incredibly good-looking estate manager. Roz does Human Resources. Brilliant, but works too hard. Stan's the Operations Manager. Stan's specialist subject on *Mastermind* would definitely be 'Everything under the Sun' – no mistakes and no passes. Ruth is our wonderful chaplain. Has a lot to say very loudly about all sorts of things, wears her spleen on her sleeve, if you know what I mean, but a sweetheart with it. And, of course, you've met Alan, our cheery, cheeky chappy of a warden. Oh, and the Congress is the group which meets every couple of months to see how things are going and to check that Alan's not run off with the petty cash again. It would be hard to forgive him a third time.'

Titters all round, but not from scowling Alan Varney.

'Couple of bishops in that group as well. Poor things can only move diagonally, but they're all right apart from that. Here we go then! We call it "The Ballad of Scarleeswanvale".'

Alison held up a sign to accompany each verse. Gerald begged a copy from her afterwards.

HOUSE
The presence of God in our toilets,
Obliterates all other scents,
Predictably so in the Ladies,
Miraculously in the Gents.

KITCHEN
The flavour of God fills our kitchen,
With spicy delights it's awash,
It gathers like praise in a glittering haze,
Divinely infusing the nosh.

FINANCE
You don't see God much down in Finance,
Asked why, he replied, 'I'll explain,
Of course I'm the King, but this is the thing,
I'm a tiny bit nervous of Jane.'

ESTATE
The estate reeks of God, but it's massive and odd,
And the manager recently groaned,
'I'm not the first Steve, I sincerely believe,
To decide I'd be better off stoned.'

HUMAN RESOURCES
Roz mentors God in the ways of HR,
Through problems that have to be faced,
Like the lady who said, with her face turning red,
'I'll not have my hormones replaced!'

HOST TEAMS
You'll never find God in the host teams,
The boredom would drive him berserk,
They're sketchily planned, and generally manned
By people who don't want to work.

CONGRESS
God must be involved in the Congress,
The whole of creation is his,
But you hit a brick wall when you study them all,
And try to guess which one he is.

OPERATIONS MANAGER
Though Stan runs divine operations,
Their scope would defy the best planner,
He has, once or twice, clamped a guest in a vice,
And adjusted his faith with a spanner.

CHAPLAINCY
Ruth is our chaplain, she's sodden with God,
And the gifts that she brings are immense,
But why does she choose to conceal all her views?
We would love her to come off the fence.

WARDEN
The warden's a fan of the Genesis God,
He wants to be like him precisely,
A long way to go, and creation is slow,
But the chaos is coming on nicely.

At the end, the whole team ran from the room waving and laughing. Lots of applause from all of us. As they passed me I distinctly heard one of the grinning girls call out with a foreign accent in a sort of stage whisper, 'Run, run, run for your lifes! Run from the warden! Run from Alan Varney while you still haf a life to lose!'

One or two of the Community members dotted around the room nearly laughed themselves sick at a couple of these verses, especially the final one. Lots of in-jokes, I expect. But Varney was furious. Seething. You could see it in his eyes. The rictus smile that he forced onto his face for the sake of 'the Guests' was deeply and hilariously un-convincing.

'There we are, then. Some of the wonderful young people in our Community!' he grated through bared teeth. 'Very independent in their choice of material, but, of course, we value them very highly, very highly indeed, and we do encourage a balance of fun and proper work.'

I said a little silent prayer asking God to deliver me from the hideous prospect of having my life balanced between fun and proper work.

Varney's 'brief reflection', which he launched into imme-diately thereafter, was alarming to say the least. Verging on disturbing. Maybe he was trying to clean away any traces of deadly flippancy that might remain in the atmosphere.

He began by dragging a horrible old pock-marked mirror in an ornate but rusty metal frame out of a Sainsbury's bag. Then he began to speak. It was like a switch being thrown on a life-size, preaching doll. His talk was a sort of verbal tsunami delivered in a hectoring, resonant voice that seemed to become more angrily Welsh as it increased in volume.

'Look at this!' he declaimed, holding the mirror up dramatically. 'What do you see? I'll tell you what you see! You see a mirror, don't you? And what do you see when you *look* in the mirror? I'll tell you what you see when you look in that mirror. YOU SEE YOURSELF!'

The force with which this rather obvious piece of information was delivered caused the front two or three rows to sway back in wide-eyed, terrified unison, like wheat assailed by a freak storm.

'And are you HAPPY with what you see in that mirror? That is my question for you this evening. ARE YOU HAPPY WITH WHAT YOU SEE?'

Wild-eyed, Varney began a sort of Groucho Marx crab-walk from one side of the room to the other, holding the mirror up so that everyone in the beleaguered front row could catch a glimpse of their troubled reflections.

'And GOD!' Varney eventually took up his position centre front once more and pointed a finger helpfully at the ceiling. 'Is GOD happy with what he sees? Every time you look at your inner mirrors this weekend, whatever you are doing at the time, I want you to ask yourselves this question. IS GOD HAPPY WITH WHAT HE SEES IN THE MIRROR OF YOUR LIVES?'

He lowered the mirror. This seemed to switch the doll off.

'Ladies and gentlemen, the next thing to happen will be hot chocolate in the other room. Goodnight.'

'Blimey!' I said to Gerald, as we trailed dismally out towards the Moon Lounge, 'if he's leading the march to heaven I think I'll drop off at Luton.'

Gerald said, 'Hmm, he does make God sound rather like a deranged Carmarthen farmer who's had his tractor stolen. Wonder what the Community thinks of him.'

Back in the Moon Lounge, while we were all chatting together and waiting for hot chocolate to arrive, the small children came in to show us what they'd been doing with Megan and Sarah. They marched in like a funeral procession, two of them holding a big paper cross covered in little coloured handprints.

'We have been looking at sin and the cross,' said the larger ghoul, her mouth moving like an expiring fish.

'Each child,' crackled the electric-shocked one, 'has placed a handprint on the paper to show that his or her sin nailed Jesus to the cross.'

The paper cross was held aloft, and greeted with a faint patter of applause for the children's sake, but, as Michael Howard's arch-critic Ann Widdecombe might have said, there was definitely something 'of the night' about these two women and their chilling pronouncement of infant guilt.

Josey stepped quietly forward and knelt down beside the little ones and their paper cross. 'I'd love it if each of you could show us which are your handprints,' she said. 'How did you do them so clearly and in such beautiful colours?'

An outbreak of chattering enthusiasm. Like spring rain in the desert. When each child had carefully identified his or her mini-masterpiece, Josey rocked back on her heels and put her finger to her lips for quiet. The little ones clustered obediently.

'When I was a bit bigger than you, but still quite little,' she said, 'guess what happened to me. I was baptised. That means that I stood in a big tank full of water, and the man who was in charge of our church said a prayer and then dipped me under the water for about two seconds before lifting me back out again. Does anyone know why he did that?'

Wide-eyed shaking of heads.

'Well, it was to show that Jesus was cleaning me up ready to have a really exciting time working for him.'

'Like a bath,' suggested a small girl with ringlets.

'*Just* like a bath,' agreed Josey, patting the little girl admiringly on her shoulder, 'cleaning me inside and outside. But I was very worried about one thing.'

'What was you worried about?' enquired a little boy, speaking around his thumb.

'Two big, grown-up men had been dipped in the tank before me, and just before they went under the water they told everyone in the church about bad things they'd done and horrible times in their lives. But I was a happy little girl, and the only bad things I could think of were silly stuff like losing my pencil or not coming straightaway when I was called. I felt a bit of a twit, but the man in charge of the church whispered that it didn't matter at all. He said Jesus was very pleased with me for letting everyone see that I wanted to belong to him, and that he knew I hadn't done anything really bad, and not to worry about it. After that I felt OK. And I was.

'When you put your lovely handprints on this paper cross earlier on, you were telling Jesus how sad you are that he got so badly hurt, and how keen you are to help him love people. Am I right? Are you keen to do that?'

Earnest nods and mumbles of agreement.

'In that case, I'm sure he wants to say thank you. Well done!'

Two minutes later, as the children broke through the invisible fence and rushed to be with their parents, Anne said quietly to me, 'Thank God for dear Josey. I'm going to join those two whether they want me or not and work with the children tomorrow.'

Too relieved to argue. Not that she would have taken any notice anyway.

Just time to sit in my bedroom on my own for a few minutes after coming back from my chat with Josey in the little chapel at the back of the house. The white wall in my room seemed so white. So very, very white. There was only one thing on it. A tiny white cross. Too small and too white to make much of a difference to all the rest of that whiteness. It was there, though. Definitely there. Something to focus on if you really looked carefully. I got a bit hypnotised by it.

I'm the only one she's told. I'm to be the strong one until we get back, and then she'll tell the others. 'How do you do that?' I asked the white cross. 'How do you do that when there is no strength in you? Some tablet you can take? A drink? One big, clever prayer?

'My sorrow is so great that it almost crushes me.'

64

We'll do this together. No indulgence. No games. No Adrian stuff. No spilling anything. Bottom out and be the strong one. Go the Nike way. The Jesus way. Just do it. OK.

There's something wrong with my pearl of great price. She might die. She might not. We might not talk about it again until we all get home. Am I willing to be silently leaned on? That's what she wanted to know.

Richard quoted the Gospel according to Winston earlier in the evening. A crudely constructed aphorism, Alan Varney called it. 'It's not enough to do our best; sometimes we have to do what is required.' Am I weak? Yes, I am. Can I do it? God knows, I can't. Am I willing? Yes, I am. Will I do it? Yes, I will.

Had to go back down to the others. People depending on me. Had to get on with it.

A voice seemed to whisper, 'Tell me about it.'

The lady called Janice from Reception came and spoke quietly to me at the foot of the stairs just before the hot chocolate arrived.

She said, 'I'm really sorry about the mix-up earlier, Mr Plass. Sandra and I are just getting used to the new booking system. It's called Chamber Master. Apparently, the person who devised it was a bit of a feminist, and she originally called it Chamber Mistress, but Alan Varney thought that didn't seem quite right for a Christian conference centre, so he changed it. Anyway, it's very complicated until you get used to it, and I'm afraid . . .' She hung her head. 'You're not going to believe this. I don't want to tell you, but – we were a whole fortnight wrong in our planning. I know that must seem impossible, and we're very ashamed and sorry, but that's what happened. So the bryologists . . .'

'The moss people? They sound like characters in one of those low-budget horror films.' She giggled.

'Yes, that's right, the moss people. They're not here this weekend. There is a schizophrenic recovery group down in our village annexe, and there's just one small extra church weekend going on in the main house, but that's it. Your two groups take up most of the beds. I really am very sorry. I don't think Mr Dekkle's going to forgive me. He glares and gnashes his teeth every time he sees me.'

'Don't worry. He might as well get some practice in while he can. Sorry, I shouldn't have said that. I think he needs a fresh expression. I'll get my son to talk to him. It must get very confusing sorting it all out. Thanks for working so hard. By the way, what's the other group?'

'Oh, they're from Swansea, quite near where the warden used to live. They come from something called the Unitarian Church.'

'Do you know what they believe?'

'I'm not sure, but Alan Varney said it was the only time he'd ever agreed with – let me see, what did he call him? I think it was "That fat little womanising drunkard of a word-cobbling con artist."'

'Mm, that would be Dylan Thomas probably. I think he grew up in Swansea. So what did Alan's favourite poet say about the Unitarians?'

'He said that Unitarians believe in one God – at most.'

'Thanks, Janice, I must ask them if he's right.'

'Yes, they seem very nice, whatever they believe in.'

She smiled as she turned to go.

'I won't say that to Alan, though.'

No, I thought to myself as Janice disappeared down the corridor behind the stairs, don't say that to Alan. I worry he's not very nice at all, whatever he believes in.

So annoying when you give people responsibility and then find that they've used it.

I asked Richard months ago to organise the Saturday evening entertainment. Told me over hot chocolate that he's allowing Cameron to organise a quiz as part of the proceedings. Very disturbing. Gerald was bad enough at the age of seventeen, but Cameron is Gerald cubed. Found Cameron playing pool by himself in the Upper Lounge and said, as casually as I could, 'Great to hear you're doing the quiz tomorrow evening, Cam. You will be sensitive when you choose the questions, won't you, old chap?'

Cameron smiled. Suddenly remembered, with a sinking heart, a friend offering me a lift on the back of his powerful motorbike when I was young. As I got on, I said, 'Don't go too fast, will you, I'm a bit nervous.' My friend turned to look at me with a terrifying, wolfish grin on his face. During the next fifteen minutes I nearly died of fear on that bike. No, actually, come to think of it, I actually, nearly, actually, physically died.

Cameron was smiling one of those same wolfish, V-shaped smiles at me now.

He said, 'Oh, yes, don't you fret, Granddad, I'll make sure every single one is something to do with the Church and God and all that. Don't you worry.'

Why am I not reassured?

Asked Anne tonight what she thought about Cameron doing the quiz.

She yawned and said, 'Oh, it'll be all right. You worry too much, there's no real harm in the boy.'

Didn't argue, but I don't agree. There *is* real harm in the boy. I always thought Gerald's sense of humour needed pruning. Cameron's doesn't just need pruning. It needs digging out by the roots and incinerating. All a little worrying. Hope it'll be all right.

Also, Richard's asked me if I'll take charge of a joke-telling slot in the middle of the entertainment. Said I would. Wish I hadn't. Oh, well, it can't be that difficult, can it?

Came down late tonight to look for a biscuit in the kitchen. Found a tall, thin rather formal looking lad of about twenty buttering some bread on the serving hatch. Got talking and asked him what he thinks of the warden.

'He's fantastic,' he said, nodding furiously, like a furiously nodding mannequin. 'As long as you work hard and stick to the rules. He's been great. Like a second father to me – more like a first father, actually. You know exactly where you are with Alan. Top bloke.'

'Good, well that's good . . .'

So, there you are then.

Shame. I prefer my villains undiluted.

Realised as I was about to get back into bed that I'd completely forgotten I put my name down for leading the workshop on Fresh Expressions tomorrow afternoon. I don't know anything about Fresh Expressions. Despite my flippant comment to Janice, I'm not even very clear what it is. Something to do with church happening in new ways, isn't it? I don't know how many times I've nodded wisely and enthusiastically when someone else has mentioned it in conversation. Spent fifteen urgent minutes doing some proogling.

Lay awake for ages after putting the light out. Nothing to distract me in the darkness. Tried to pray, but prayer doesn't take away the job that has to be done. Everything in me was screaming to tell Anne about Josey. I'm not allowed, so I couldn't. Didn't.

5

Saturday Morning

Woken by my phone going at 6 o'clock this morning. First time it's had any reception since we've been here. Leonard calling, from – well, somewhere in the British Isles (presumably). Sounded quite faint.

I said, 'Leonard, why are you calling me at this time of the morning? Are you getting any nearer?'

'No, not really, we got up early to get a good start as soon as the ferry came in, but I need . . .'

'The *ferry*? What are you doing on a ferry? A *ferry*! Which ferry?'

'From somewhere to somewhere else I think. I'm not sure. I wanted some advice.'

'Yes?'

'Well, we got onto the main road OK in the end, but we've nearly had several accidents. The SatNav keeps saying, "Turn around when possible," but it's really dangerous to do that while you're driving along because you can't see what's happening on the road ahead. Do you think it would be all right for Angels to do the turning round when Katy says that, or does it have to be the actual driver?'

Seem to remember reading somewhere that extreme lateral thinkers make up for the negative effects of their strange perspectives by displaying creative ability in other areas of their lives. That ought to put Thynn roughly on a par with Leonardo Da Vinci. No actual sign of the creative brilliance emerging so far, though. Explained that the SatNav meant they were going the wrong way and needed to turn the car round and go in the other direction as soon as it was possible and safe to do so.

'Not on the motorway, though, surely?'

'Oh, my God, *no*! No, of course not, Leonard!'

Heard them both laughing raucously.

'Only joking, Adrian! Got you there, didn't we? We're not stupid, you know!

Oh, good – I'm glad they're not stupid . . .

As Anne came out of the shower this morning she asked if I'd managed to get a good night's sleep.

I blustered, 'Oh, yes, well, I was a bit worried about this Fresh Expressions workshop, so I spent a while proogling. Felt a lot better after that.'

'I see. And am I allowed to know what that means, or would you rather keep it to yourself until you get a chance to talk it through with your male friends?'

'Proogling,' I explained with appropriate dignity, 'is a word that Gerald, *your* son, made up. It's a cross between praying and googling. Useful when you're feeling ignorant about something.'

'Right, I've got it. So you know all about Fresh Expressions now, do you, sweetheart?'

'No, I know enough to sound like someone who probably knows a lot more, but has decided to let others have a go rather than show off.'

'My goodness,' said Anne, towelling her hair, 'you do

make hard work of life sometimes, don't you? By the way, who was that on the phone at some awful hour?'

'Oh, right, that was Leonard. They're completely lost. About to get on a ferry, would you believe?'

'Yes,' said Anne sadly, 'I'm afraid I would . . .'

Today is the day when we have our silent meal at lunchtime. Despite everything I'm really looking forward to seeing if Mountainberger's right about love, grace and spiritual harmony and all the rest of it.

Got talking on the way down this morning to a young female Community member called Beth, who was limply flicking the banisters with a dusting cloth. Asked her why she was looking so sad.

'Got told off by the warden this morning for being late at the team prayer meeting.'

Her eyes filled with tears.

'He really had a go at me in front of all the others. It was horrible.'

'Why were you late?'

'My mum phoned to say that my sister went into hospital last night because she had one of her really bad fits. She was crying on the phone. I couldn't just leave her, could I?'

'Why didn't you tell the warden about your sister?'

'I did try. I went up to whisper to him, but he shouted at me to sit down and think about the fact that I'd held everybody up. I don't think he likes me very much.' She sniffed unhappily. 'I want to go home.'

'Will you go home?'

Beth smiled damply.

'No, I'll be all right. I'm off shift this afternoon. I'll borrow one of the dogs and go for a walk with my music. Thank you for being nice.'

Came across patient Sally on the patio outside the Moon Lounge, sitting on all her things and drinking coffee. Asked her how she got on last night.

She said, 'I ended up eventually in a bunk in some sort of annexe down in the village with a load of other people. I didn't really mind. They seemed fairly nice, you know, but a bit strange. Quite a lot of them asked what medication I was on. Don't know why. Anyway, my top bunk was a bit short and my feet were hanging over the end, so I went to bed with my socks on because of the cold, and when I woke up in the morning everyone had gone, and one of my socks was missing.

She stared sadly into the distance for a moment.

'You know, I spent quite a long time hunting for that sock. Then I discovered that someone must have taken one of my socks off and put it on over the other one. Strange. I suppose it was a sort of joke. I don't really mind, but . . .'

Sat opposite Dennis at breakfast. Said nonchalantly as I buttered toast, 'Dennis, old chap, small point, I was just wondering whether it's worth us trying to fit the plenary session in before everyone goes home, seeing as we have so much to get through. What do you think?'

He waved aside a bevy of honey-coloured dancing girls with a gesture and said, with unusual enthusiasm and energy, 'Well, Adrian, if you're asking me, I'd say it was crucial. Absolutely crucial. In my experience the Holy

Spirit really uses these plenary sessions. People's lives can be transformed. Let's *make* it happen!'

I punched the air feebly and said, 'Right! Right! Yes! Transformed. We want that! We'll – we'll make it happen . . .'

Having no sense of humour can be very dangerous some-times – for the person who suffers from that deficiency, I mean. If I'd been Alan Varney at the end of breakfast this morning I would never have read out the list of forthcoming events that some brave person had added to the official programme on the main notice board. Holding the offending document in one hand and the microphone in the other, he sounded like the local minister announcing a major pit disaster as he started to speak.

'I am very sorry to have to tell you this, but some person or persons unknown have seen fit to affix a sheet of paper to the official notice board detailing events in our programme that are not actually scheduled. I have removed the said document, but to avoid possible confusion I should warn our guests that the following projected items have no basis in fact. They will not be happening. They do not exist. The individual or individuals concerned may have committed this anonymous indiscretion with humorous intent, but I am quite sure that our guests will *not* be amused.'

As Varney shook the sheet of paper in his hand to straighten it out, I almost felt sorry for him.

'These are the items in question,' he continued.

Poor old Alan. He could not have been more wrong about guests failing to find the 'anonymous indiscretion' funny. People were in stitches by the time he was halfway through the third description. Realising this at last, he stopped reading and grimly announced that a list of genuine events was available in the printed programme, thus provoking expressions of disappointment from many of those present. One or two were wiping tears from their eyes. By means that I am not prepared to divulge even in the privacy of this journal, I was able to obtain a copy of this interesting list in its entirety. It reads as follows.

GUIDED RETREAT

Women drivers – come and have your spatial awareness pampered by experts. Double parking facilities available for all guests.

POSITIVELY ADULTEROUS

Why do church people get so gloomy and negative about adultery? This week we shall be looking at the lighter side of infidelity, heartbreak and treachery. Please bring along your funny stories, and let's have a laugh together! (Alan Varney will be away.)

RENEW, REFRESH AND RESTORE

An exciting three-day opportunity for guests to be renewed, refreshed and restored. After feedback from the last event of this kind we are offering additional choices. Those who are already refreshed and restored can now become renewed on the first day of the course, while those who are renewed and restored but in need of refreshment can attend the second day. Those who wish to renew their refreshment and restoration should book for the second and third days of the event, and any who are anxious to renew the restoration of their refreshment or the refreshment of their restoration should put their names down for the second half of the first session of the renewal day, and the first half of the second session of the restoration day respectively. Please state your requirements clearly on the forms provided. Please note that Alan Varney is no longer available to lead the course owing to stress.

HOW TO BE A WARM AND ENCOURAGING LEADER

Alan Varney has spent twenty years in leadership. He will be sharing his relationship skills and insights in this short course (course duration: almost five minutes). Please be on time as Alan has a very short fuse.

A VERY HELPFUL WEEKEND

Are you middle-class, set in your ways and reluctant to face challenge in your Christian walk? If so, this could be the event for you. In the course of this weekend we shall be looking at simple and enjoyable ways to embed ourselves firmly and guiltlessly into the comfort of compromise. Session titles will include:

HOW MUCH SHOULD WE GIVE? – FINDING A
 WORKABLE BALANCE
OUTREACH IN CHALLENGING SITUATIONS
 – PROTECTING THE TEMPLE OF THE HOLY
 SPIRIT
MARTYRDOM – WHO DOES IT *REALLY*
 HELP?

FORGIVENESS – DRAWING LINES THAT
  WORK FOR US
COMMITMENT TO THE CHURCH – A SUBTLE
  RECIPE FOR NEGLECT?
THE ATONEMENT – A PECULIARLY JEWISH
  VIEW OF THE CRUCIFIXION AND
  RESURRECTION?

Previous participants have described this course as 'very helpful', and many have made a number of return visits. Do book early to avoid encouragement.

CATERING FOR THE MARGINALISED

Here at Scarleeswanvale we always like to set aside at least one week each year for marginalised or minority groups in the Church. This year we are thrilled to be welcoming delegates from NECF, the Naturist Embroiderers' Christian Fellowship. This is the second time we have hosted NECF members, and we shall be offering a programme similar to the last one, except that, on this occasion, biscuits will not be served to guests in any public space within the confines of the building.

Went into the Reception Office a bit later to pay for some chocolate I'd taken from the little shop in the hall. Alan Varney on his own, sitting at the desk. As I put a five pound note into the cash box and counted out my change, I said casually, 'Must be really tough doing your job, Alan. All these different personalities trying to cope with being one Community.'

Replied, but didn't bother to look up.

'Cope? There's no *cope* about it. They make promises to God when they come, and my job is to make sure that they keep them.'

'What about when they get unhappy and are having trouble keeping their promises?'

'We have prayer triplets set up to deal with personal problems, and two chaplains, clergy and lay, who are always available. Now, if you don't mind, I am very busy.'

Hovered for a moment, wondering if there was anything else I ought to say.

'The thing is, Alan, some of the Community members think you're wonderful. But, if you don't mind me saying so, one or two I've spoken to are very unsure and quite miserable. Did you know that? They feel disapproved of. See themselves as failures in your eyes – and God's. One of them said you blasted at her and made her cry in front of the others when she was late for some meeting, and you refused to listen when she tried to explain what had happened.'

Varney laid his pen down on the desk, and moved into his LOOK-INTO-THIS-MIRROR mode.

'Two things, Mr Plass. First of all, I never listen to gossip . . .'

'I don't think you could describe . . .'

'And, nor, if I may say so, should you. Secondly, I have been employed by God and by the Scarleeswanvale Congress to bring shape and order back into this organisation. That is my commitment and that is precisely what I am going to do. Good morning to you.'

I tidied up my papers and turned towards the door. I really wanted to say, 'Alan, has anyone ever told you that you have an excessively pointed head?' But I didn't. I said, 'Alan, you make me feel very sad,' just loudly enough for him to hear and quietly left the office.

Decided to step outside for a couple of minutes before the first morning session began. Was leaning against one of the massive stone pillars that hold up the porch when Minnie Stamp came tripping like a mobile daisy across the gravel from her car, a lilac cardigan folded across her arm. My heart sank. Decided that, this time, I would say nothing that could be remotely construed as referring to a personal problem. Just a matter of selecting the right words, surely. She stopped in front of me, adjusted her feet into the first position, crinkled her eyes, and placed her head at its optimum counselling angle. Felt my toes curling.

'Adrian. Are you nervy-chops about going into the scary old session thingy all on your ownsome?'

Hold your nerve. Casual but firm.

'No, Minnie, I'm not at all scared. I'm actually really looking forward to Stanley Blorgan's talk. I've only stepped outside for a moment or two. I just – need some air.'

'Oh, have you got a respiratory problem, Adrian?'

So annoyed that I drew a deep breath in, and then – damn it – I coughed as I let it out.

'No, Minnie,' I replied after clearing my throat, 'I haven't got a respiratory problem. I'm fine. I'm just getting a little . . .'

'Have you seen a doctor recently, Adrian?'

'No, because there's no . . .'

'Adrian, you're a man, aren't you?'

Stared at her.

79

'Yes, Minnie, I am a man. What's that got to do with it?'

'Men are *so* scaredy-cat about going along to the surgery. Adrian, you have to be a brave little soldier.'

She fixed me with one of her ghastly insightful stares.

'You won't have to take your knick-knacks off, you know. Not if it's a respiratory disease. Is that what you're afraid of, Adrian, that you'll have to take your knick-knacks off?'

For goodness *sake*!

'Minnie, I'm not afraid of . . .'

'No one's going to need to see your little personal bits, Adrian, not if it's a respiratory disease. Respiratory diseases can be really serious, Adrian. *Go* to the doctor.'

Gave in as usual, just to put an end to this excruciating conversation.

'All right, all right! I'll go! I'll go to the doctor. Thank you. I'll go.'

'Do you want to lean on me as we go into the session, Adrian? That'll save you breathing so much.'

'No, no, you go on ahead, Minnie. I'll stay here for a moment and – and breathe some of this nice clean air.'

'All right, Adrian. Remember, I love you.' She raised a forefinger in mock reprimand. 'Not in a Romeo and Juliet, making children, kissy-cuddling way, but like a radiant angel loves a very special little sunbeam.'

Blew me a kiss (which I managed to mentally duck) and disappeared into the house.

Felt as if the inside of my head had been beaten up. I seem to recall that lawyers in French courts during the nineteenth century were able to argue a defence of *crime passionnel* when major crimes were committed in a sudden, overwhelming fit of rage. Shame it's not available in England nowadays. There's not a jury on earth that wouldn't acquit me if I was accused of murdering Minnie Stamp after the conversation I'd just endured. Justifiable homicide. That would cover it.

Couldn't face going into the session after that. Wandered down to a little covered wooden shelter beside a small lake on the distant edge of the big sloping lawn. To my surprise Josey was in there, staring out across the water. Sat down beside her. She jumped a little, then patted my knee and laughed.

'Not going in, Adrian? You'll be in trouble. You're supposed to be organising the whole thing. Well, if you're playing hookey, come and play hookey with me. I'd like that.'

Told her all about my encounter with Minnie. She laughed and laughed. So did I in the end.

'But why me, Josey? Why on earth does she always home in on me?'

'Difficult to say. Maybe she feels sorry for you. I think it's that little sad elf look of yours.'

She went into peals of laughter again.

'Anne told you.'

'Of course. We tell each other everything.'

'Everything?'

Pause.

'Most things, yes.'

'Right! She's for it.'

After that we sat in silence for at least a couple of minutes. Then Josey leaned her face against my shoulder and began to sob silently. I put my arm around her and waited, praying that if there was anything I ought to say I would get it half right. Several tissues later she spoke in a very small, snuffly voice.

'Can I explain why I haven't told them yet?'

'If you want to.'

'Thing is – I only got the call-back from the surgery just before we left. Hours before. The doctor wanted me in first thing Monday morning. When I asked if it could be later in the week her voice changed. Sort of urgent and insistent. Decisions might have to be made, she said. I didn't like that. So frightening. I had a friend . . .'

Her voice trailed away.

'I've been trying to tell myself that it might be nothing much, but I know it could turn out to be something – something really nasty. The thing is, though, that I didn't – don't know anything for sure, so I decided not to tell Gerald until we get back. He's so – so jolly hopeful and excited about what this weekend might do for the church. He's worked so *hard*, Adrian. And he cares so much. So . . .'

'Is that the only reason?'

'Oh, no.'

She sat up against the back of her seat and stared across the surface of the lake again, still dabbing at her eyes.

'There are some things you can never take back. Not ever. Not after you've let them go. Once you've seen people's faces crumple and change and fill up with pain you can't go back two seconds or two minutes or two hours or however long it's been. You can't say, "Give me back that horrible thing I said earlier on. I'll pack it carefully away and we'll all pretend we never saw it or said it or heard it in the first place." You can't do that. You really can't, Adrian.'

She shifted her weight suddenly as though a sharp pain had passed through her body.

'I suppose I'm just frightened of facing the moment when I have to be the one who fires words like – like bullets right into the very middle of their hearts. One moment they'll be OK. Then they won't. Horrible. Horribly huge. I can see their faces. And I'll be the one who does it to them.'

'Why did you decide to tell me?'

Josey turned and looked directly at me, her eyes wide with the need to convey exactly what she meant.

'You're my friend. Telling you is like – telling me.'

Some kind of Olympic stadium. Possibly thousands of people there, but not a solitary word, not the slightest rustle of movement. I am on the podium to receive a gold medal for being Josey's friend. Never trained, never expected to be awarded anything, never even put my name down for the race, if that's what it was. The gold medal! Who would have thought it? But I would return it without a word if it meant that Josey could outlive me.

'When we go home after the weekend, will you and Anne come up on Monday so that you can both be there when I tell the others? I shall know by then.'

I shook my head.

'Sorry, Josey, there are limits, you know.'

She sat up and started punching me rhythmically on the shoulder.

'You and Gerald should be stranded on a little desert island together. That way you can both be sure of finding at least one other person who shares your sense of humour.'

At the end of the final punch her small fist stayed for a moment on my shoulder.

83

'Thank you, Adrian.'

'Pleasure, Josey.'

We sat in silence for quite a long time after that. The air was completely still, and for as far as I could see nothing ruffled the surface of the lake.

Very disturbing moment at coffee time. Anne came up with a smile on her face and whispered in my ear.

'Adrian, I've heard all about the serious illness.'

Felt the blood drain from my face. Why was she smiling? How *could* Anne smile about something so awful and frightening?

'She told you?'

'Yes, at some length. I thought I'd never get away. Drove me mad. I told her I had to go to the loo in the end. She came with me and talked from the next stall. She's unstoppable.'

The mist began to clear.

'Oh, you mean . . .'

'Apparently you've got a severe respiratory illness, probably viral pneumonia, but you won't go for treatment because you're frightened of having to take your knick-knacks off in front of the doctor. First I've heard of this.'

'And the last. In the end I had to go along with Minnie's nonsense just to stop her drivelling on. Tell me something, Anne. Do you love me in a Romeo and Juliet, making children, kissy-cuddling way, or like a radiant angel loves a very special little sunbeam?'

Anne laughed out loud.

'Hmm, let's think. Never was a story of such woe as J and her R. Don't fancy that. Certainly won't be making any more children, not that I'm involved in anyway. You and your second wife might. Presumably the angel-sunbeam thing is Minnie and you. I think I'd go for the kissy-cuddling option, my darling. Did you have something special in mind?'

'No – I mean, yes! Yes, I'd definitely go for that option as well. And I've always got something in mind . . .'

Asked Gerald at coffee time how he thought the first session had gone.

He sighed and said, 'Hmm, it ended a lot better than it started. At least, I think it was better. What happened to you, by the way? Did you get lost?'

'Me? Er, no, I just felt a bit worn out with it all. Went and – and played hookey with Josey. It was nice to spend time with her.'

'Oh, that's all right, then. She'll have enjoyed that. She's never been very keen on people blethering on for an hour.'

'What were you going to say about the session? What was wrong with the first bit?'

He sighed.

'Well, what's that line from Francis of Assisi that everyone's always quoting nowadays? "Preach the gospel always – use PowerPoint if necessary." Remember that one?'

'Er, yes – something a bit like that.'

'Well, it's a pity this Blorgan fellow didn't take the hint. I've never seen anything like it. He didn't miss an opportunity. "Good morning, everybody!" Large crowing cockerel appears, followed by a clip of the sun rising, just in case the obscure concept of morning is one that eludes us. Thirty seconds later, "I hope you've all got your Bibles with you." Big close-up of – you'll never guess what!'

'A Bible?'

'Yes, a Bible, presumably to prevent any of us confused males dragging *Lady Chatterley's Lover* out of our Christian man-bags by mistake. "We're going to be looking at the story of the Widow of Nain, which you will find in the seventh chapter of Luke's Gospel in your clanky, old, steam-powered, hand-operated Bibles."'

'He didn't say that last bit.'

'No, he didn't. He's quite a good speaker, but he doesn't really do humour. I just made that up. Anyway, at that point the screen goes berserk. Bible reference, alternative transla-tions, pictures of present-day widows, drawings of contem-porary widows, map showing where Nain is now, map showing where Nain probably was then, cartoon of crowds and dead son and widow and Jesus and disciples and – can't remember the rest. What a click-fest! That man must have one very fit and over-developed thumb.'

'And then it got better?'

'No, then it got worse. After a bit more chat Blorgan said that before we went any further we needed to have a time of confession so that we could be clean sheets on which the Holy Spirit might write.'

'You mean he got everyone to say a prayer of confession together?'

'No, no, that would have been fine. No, he made us get into groups of three so that – wait for it – we could each confess to something *shameful* in our lives.'

'Goodness gracious! Did he use that actual word?'

'Yes, that was it. Something shameful.'

'And who were you with?'

A wry smile passed across Gerald's face.

'O-o-o-oh! I was faced with the extraordinary prospect of confessing something shameful to Alvin Dekkle and Mrs Danby-Carstairs – she's the large, grim-looking lady from our church. Imagine it! Both of them spend most of their time talking about everyone else getting things wrong. She was sitting grimly in her chair like a pile of pillow-shaped granite boulders encased in wool, and he was slumped back, pendulum-ing his heavy head from side to side like a motorist who's been cut up on a roundabout, presumably to advertise his terminal despair over the whole proceedings. I have to confess, Dad – in my less holy moments I consider both of them prime candidates for the giant blender and, now that I think about it, perhaps that's actually the most shameful thing in my life. Jesus loves everyone, but if he was truly man when he walked this earth there must have been some individuals who got right up his nose. How did he resist the temptation to dump them – in love? "Peter, I've had as much as I can stand of that bloke over there. Just give me a hand dropping him down the nearest well, will you? Cheers, mate."'

'Gosh, I'm reeling from the thought of the bitter paste that would result from those two being blended. Gerald, you didn't confess you wanted to do that, did you? You're a braver man than me if you did.'

'Good heavens, no. Come o-o-on! That would have been the truth, and you know what happens to the Church when the truth creeps in. All hell breaks loose.'

'I thought it was supposed to set us free.'

He patted my arm.

'Now, Dad, you don't want to go believing everything you read, do you? Or rather, you don't want to believe any

87

one thing without reference to all the other things. Ask Father John, he'll tell you. We Jesus-loving relativists have got to follow the Master. Float like a butterfly, sting like a bee, shrewd as snakes, innocent as doves, and all that.'

'I think you might have got a bit of Mohammed Ali mixed up in there.'

'Have I? Oh, excellent.'

'So what did you confess to?'

'Well, what I confessed to was true enough, but kind of strategic as well, if you know what I mean. Not that the strategy worked in the end. I wound my fingers together, dropped my hands down between my knees, and hung my head like a Sally Army penitent on the mercy seat. I was *so* vulnerable. Tell you what, I was so incredibly humble that I nearly had to confess to pride. Then I said, "Veronica and Alvin, I want to confess to God and to you that I have often been guilty of failing to make an effort to understand the views of those who don't think in the same way as me. I would like to ask God's forgiveness, and yours specifically, if you feel that I've let you down in that way. Please be gracious enough to forgive me."

'Then I stayed there, head bowed, determined that I wouldn't move a muscle until someone said something.'

'And what happened?'

'Oh, probably the most annoying thing I could possibly have imagined. Dekkle laid a hand on my shoulder, drew a breath in through pursed lips like a mechanic spotting a fault in a malfunctioning car, and said, "My man," (My man!) "it's all about listening. It's all about really listening to what the other person is saying. That's what it's about. You have to learn how to listen. That's what people really need." From that moment onwards I wasn't able to get a word in edgeways because he was too busy lecturing me on the need to listen. Nearly drove me bonkers.'

'So did either of them confess to anything shameful?'

'When Alvin ran out of breath and I finally had a chance to ask if he'd done anything he was ashamed of, he confessed to wearing himself out by being too constantly open and available to the needs of others. "Too much like Jesus." I think those were his exact words.'

'And Mrs Danby-Carstairs?'

'Oh, yes. After a little careful thought she confessed with glittering eyes to disliking Alvin Dekkle more than anyone else she'd ever met in the entire course of her life. You can imagine what a jolly little threesome we were after that. The other groups were deep in prayer, all leaning inwards with their eyes closed and their heads tilted to one side, as per normal. We three were slumped miserably in our own little worlds hoping that planet Earth would explode in the very near future. Dreadful!'

'But something good happened later on, you said.'

The rueful smile faded from Gerald's face.

'Well, yes, it did, but I can't really pin down what it was. I think it was good – potentially, but I'm not sure what that's going to mean. This Blorgan fellow said he wanted us to sit in silence for five minutes and concentrate on one sentence from the passage. It was up on the screen, of course.'

'What was the sentence?'

'It was part of verse thirteen. "His heart went out to her." Those were the six words we had to concentrate on. So I sat there, trying to let the meaning of it all sink in, and suddenly – I don't quite know how to put this – it was as though that phrase was getting branded on to my – well, my heart I suppose.'

'Painfully?'

'Not exactly. A sort of benevolent scorching, if that means anything. It got written, and I couldn't rub it out now if I wanted to. What do you make of it, Dad? If you were Lucy van Pelt and I was Charlie Brown you'd tell me I was cracking up. Can you think of anything special that ties in with those words?'

Shook my head slowly, trying to think of something to say. Memory flashed. Black clouds rolling over the hills above Wharfedale in North Yorkshire one late afternoon when, as a skinny, rucksack-laden teenager, I found myself tramping wearily towards food and sleep at a Youth Hostel in Kettlewell, a village that never seemed to come any closer however far and fast I walked. The storm caught me just before I began the descent off the tops, terrifying me to the point of humiliation with its mindless, hammering power. I did reach my bunker in the end, but the frenzied, pitiless force of the storm in contrast with my own cowering insig-nificance stayed with me for the rest of my life. Storms happen. Black clouds bring them.

'I suppose the best thing is just to hang on to – you know, the way you're feeling and the words themselves, and see if they fit in with something in the future. Just – wait and see,' I concluded lamely.

Gerald nodded and said, 'Yes, I suppose you're right. Yes, I'll do that. I'll wait and see. Thanks, Dad.'

Overheard a conversation between Cameron and Richard Cook just before the second session began. Amazing. It could have been Gerald talking to Richard twenty-five years ago.

Cameron said, 'Oh, Uncle Richard, I meant to say to you – I'd never realised before this morning's worship session that God is an expert goalkeeper.'

Richard knit his brows and stared at Cameron in bewilderment. I know I get drawn into nonsense occasionally, but Richard is in a class of his own. He never did learn. He never does learn. He never will learn.

'I'm sorry, Cameron, I don't remember anything from this morning about God being a goalkeeper or any kind of footballer at all.'

'It was in the middle of one of the choruses, Uncle Richard. You know, the one that goes:

> You are the everlasting God
> The everlasting God
> You do not feint. You won't grow weary
> You're the defender of the week
> You comfort those in need
> You lift us up on wings like eagles . . .

'See what I mean? Someone's voted him Defender of the Week. He must have had a really good game on Saturday. Obviously encouraged the rest of the players no end. Doesn't even need to feint. When you play like that without showing how tired you're getting it gives the others a real lift, on wings like eagles, in fact.'

Richard stared at my wicked grandson for a full five seconds before a light came on in his face. Not much brighter than a Toc H lamp, as my grandfather used to say, but a light nevertheless. He tapped the table with his coffee spoon as he spoke.

'Ah! I think I've spotted the problem, Cameron. You see, I think you must have assumed that the word was spelled "w-e-e-k", whereas actually it was spelled "w-e-a-k", which means something completely different. Do you understand what I mean?'

'Oh, I get it,' replied Cameron innocently. 'How silly of me.' Nodded thoughtfully for a moment. 'It's a shame, though, isn't it, Uncle Richard.'

'A shame?'

'Yes, it's a shame God doesn't play in goal for England, don't you think?'

'Er yes, I suppose so. Why?'

'Well, we might win some of those penalty shoot-offs we do so badly at.'

'Might we?'

'Yes, just imagine!' He stretched his hands out as far as they'd go on both sides of his body. 'We'd have a keeper with everlasting arms.'

Cameron quietly stood and picked up his empty coffee mug to return it to the counter, leaving Richard staring into space, his mouth twitching as he silently mouthed that final sentence. Might take a couple of days . . .

Only one memory of Richard deliberately making a joke, and it was rather a bitter one. We were both at a Saturday morning talk for men about 'Christian Marriage', led by a man with about a thousand very white teeth and a transatlantic accent. I sensed fairly early on that Richard was finding the whole thing pretty meaningless. At one point this smooth operator talked in his meat-jelly voice about ways of brightening up our approach to love-making.

'Why not have a pillow-fight?' he burbled. 'There's more than one kind of foreplay.'

Richard didn't say anything, but he turned his head and looked at me briefly with raised eyebrows. I could guess what he was thinking. First of all, the chances of his sewn-up wife Doreen ever agreeing to such a wild plan were about one in a trillion. Secondly, if she ever did, by some miracle, go along with the idea, the exchange would have to involve old, discoloured pillows taken down from the loft for the purpose, and conducted with passionless decorum, each pillow needing to be retrieved after its individual, floppy Frisbee flight and carefully smoothed before another sedate launch could be risked.

It was a little after this that Richard actually made a comment out loud. Meat-jelly man had been talking about the importance of a physical relationship in marriage.

'There are no rules,' he said fleshily, 'but one would hope that Christian husbands and wives might honour their wedding vows to each other and to God by regularly engaging in physical union. *Is that your experience?*'

'Oh, yes,' muttered Richard in a deadened voice, 'regular as clockwork since we married forty years ago. Once every decade – without fail.'

Had a really good chat with the attractive, dark-haired girl who was so nice to Gladys at dinner. Her name is Karina. She comes from Latvia and is working here at Scarleeswanvale for a year before going back home to carry on with her degree course. Had a bit of a laugh about finding rhymes for unusual English words. Nice girl.

*　　　*　　　*

Went into the second session. People said afterwards that it was interesting and useful, but I hardly heard a word. Kept thinking about Gerald and Cameron and Anne, and picturing their faces when they heard the news, whatever that turns out to be. Made me shiver.

At one point, though, glancing through the window, I was temporarily distracted by the sight of Sally, the co-operative volunteer, out in the grounds in the distance trailing her bags and bedclothes along towards a small summerhouse on the edge of the back lawn. When she pulled the door open a veritable downpour of long-handled garden tools rained down on her unresisting, bowed figure. Watched her patiently picking up all the tools and carefully replacing them in the summerhouse before gathering her own stuff together again and limping mournfully away across the lawn. I know she says she doesn't really mind, but . . .

Round of applause for Stanley Blorgan at the end of his second and final session. Well received generally despite his overactive PowerPoint gland. Gave him a cheque, thanked him very much on behalf of everyone and shook his hand. Didn't stay for lunch. So many teeth!

Rather alarmed to find a message in my pigeon-hole from the warden asking me to see him before lunch to explain my reasons for seriously insulting Karina, the nice Latvian girl I chatted with earlier. Had no idea what this meant! How could I have upset her? Showed Anne the note.

She said, 'Oh, Adrian, for goodness sake, what on earth have you done to the poor girl?'

I said indignantly, 'What do you mean by that? I haven't *done* anything to the *poor* girl. She's not a poor girl. What do you think I might have *done*? All I did was try to help her with her English. Honestly!'

Bit nervous of meeting with the warden. I hadn't enjoyed any of my encounters with Alan Varney so far. I suspected that this one was unlikely to go any better than the others. I had a feeling he would enjoy finding a reason to shout at me after my comment this morning. Happened to meet one of the older, more grizzled members of the Estate Team outside the front door just as coffee time was ending. Said casually, 'You must have been around for a while. What sort of guy is the warden? What's your take on him?'

He snarled Scottishly and said, 'They've all been cr-r-r-rap except fer-r-r one! This one's nae sae bad sae long as he's nae allowed to pr-r-r-reach under-r-r-r the fire alur-r-r-rums. The hot air-r-r sets 'em off.'

I suppose that was meant to be a joke, but he didn't smile.

Frustratingly scratchy telephone call from Leonard just as I was on my way to see the warden.
    'Hello, is that Adrian?
    'Yes, yes, where are you now, Leonard?'
    'Yes.'
    'WHERE ARE YOU NOW?'
    'Oh, I'm afraid we've been a bit delayed.'
    'Well, where are you now?'
    'No, not really.'
    'I SAID – I *SAID*, WHERE ARE YOU NOW?'
    'Oh – in a hedge.'

'A HEDGE? WHAT DO YOU MEAN *IN* A HEDGE? YOU MEAN NEXT TO A HEDGE – BESIDE A HEDGE? NEAR A HEDGE?'

'No, *in* a hedge. Just a minute – ah, jolly jumpers all round! We've come out of the hedge.'

'Good! What – so you're in a lane or a street or something, are you?'

'Just before lunch.'

'No, are you – ARE YOU IN A LANE OR SOME-THING?'

'No, a field. We're in a – a sort of ploughed field. We're going to switch over to the Irishman. Angels thinks men are probably better at fields.'

'Leonard, can't you see that it doesn't make a scrap of difference whether it's a man or a – hello! Hello! LEONARD? LEONARD, ARE YOU STILL THERE . . .?'

Retired exhausted to find some Strepsils. Do hope they get here before we all leave . . .

Arrived at the Warden's Office at 12.45. Karina was sitting in the corner dabbing her eyes with a hankie. Varney had a righteous glare up and running to greet me with.

He said, 'So, Mr Plass, I gather that this young, vulnerable girl from a distant land is very upset because you found it necessary to comment on the marital status of her parents.'

Gasped in horror. My legs almost gave way. 'What! I did not! I never . . .!'

Karina sniffed and swallowed.

'Yes, yes, you dit! You say that my marther ant my farther are not proper to be marrit. You haf use bad worm about me.'

She held out a small square of paper with a word written in large capitals in the centre, and a note underneath saying that it was from me.

'You spent me this newt, no?'

'Spent you . . .? *Sent* you this *note* – yes, yes, I sent you that note, but this is *not* a bad word.'

Karina gasped and looked at me open-mouthed, clearly scandalised by what she saw as a blatant untruth. Got a bit desperate at this point.

'Look, you *must* remember, Karina, we were talking about English words that rhyme with "custard", and you said "mustard", and I said that was very good and I'd try to think if there were any more and I remembered that there was a bird called a "bustard", so I left you a note in your pigeon-hole about it . . .'

'In my pigeon . . .?'

'In your – never mind. Too many birds. Look, I left you a note and – and this is it. A bustard is a bird. Honestly!' Flapped my arms feebly as I spoke. 'It's a bird. It really, really is . . .'

All sorted out in the end. Karina's fine now, but it was all a bit exhausting. Oh, dear!

I think Alan was a bit disappointed that he wasn't able to throw me to the more aggressive members of the Community pack to be torn limb from limb. Did I mention I haven't taken to Alan Varney?

Told Anne in passing about my meeting with Alan Varney and Karina. She stared at me before hurrying on and said something under her breath. Sounded like, 'You stupid bustard!'

*   *   *

On a shelf just inside the Sun Room as you come past the Reception window there's a book called *God's House on the Hill: A Brief History of Scarleeswanvale* by Brenda Fittit. It's not that brief. I'd picked it up on Friday and had a flick through. It's a heavy old brick of a book, filled, as far as I could tell, with dense blocks of print describing in tediously saccharine detail the (apparently) uninterrupted joy experienced by every man, woman, animal, insect and microbe who ever passed through the gates of the conference centre.

Gerald stopped me as I was about to go out for a breath of air after my run-in with Alan. He was grinning and holding a slip of paper.

'Look at this, Dad. Looks like the "anonymous indiscretion with humorous intent", that Alan Varney got so cross about yesterday, isn't the first time someone's felt the need to embellish the official line . . . I found this just now. It was just slipped into the back of Brenda's ghastly book. Do you think we should put it back? I can't decide. Well, I'll leave it with you.'

Sat on the wall outside and read the paragraph printed on the slip.

ADDENDUM CONCERNING THE WARDENSHIP OF JONATHAN HARVESON.
BY A COMMUNITY MEMBER WHO HAS BEEN AT SCARLEESWANVALE SINCE 1763

In 20** [unreadable] we were blessed by the arrival of a new warden, Jonathan Harveson, who with his wife Beryl and his friends Vaughn and Stella Burton *introduced many fresh and valuable Scarleeswanvale traditions. Friday evenings, for instance, were to become earmarked as a deeply precious time when the warden and a small number of trusted friends might leave the confines of the estate to seek inspiration and enlightenment in a place where, as Jonathan himself so beautifully expressed it, there was a 'continual outpouring'. And what a profound encouragement it was for many of us to spot the members of this little group returning two or three hours later, faces shining with an almost unearthly glow, voices uplifted in laughter and joyful song as they wove their way up the drive, clinging to each other and to nearby trees with divinely fuelled exuberance.*

One very special personal memory. I can testify that, on one of these occasions, I witnessed the warden prostrating himself, face down on the gravel surface, as though kissing the very foundations of our communal endeavour. Indeed, so overwhelmed did he appear by the weight and symbolic significance of this experience that he literally lost the use of his legs, his companions being obliged to lift his inert form and carry it to the front door of the warden's residence.

How well I recall sitting later that evening on the hillside overlooking the river, a stretch of water so playfully (though perhaps slightly strangely) nicknamed 'Shift Creek' by the warden after two weeks in his new post. Above my head a million stars filled the sky like a vast throng of angels, and from Jonathan and Beryl's house, borne faintly on the night breeze, it was still possible to hear bursts of merriment, sudden boisterous shouts of joy, snatches of what must have been choruses from Mission Praise, *and the occasional clink of milk bottles or mugs as coffee was prepared and served. Such devotion to mutual ministry and spontaneous worship at the end of a long week said one thing very clearly to me. Scarleeswanvale could not be in better hands!*

We did hear that there had been difficult times here in the recent past. Maybe we now know a little more about what might have caused that. No, surely not!

6

Saturday Afternoon

Silent meal finished half an hour ago. All I can say is that the membership of Denver Mountainberger's church must be made up of deaf mutes, expert mime artists and children with their hands tied behind their backs and mouths gagged. Partly my own fault. Whatever possessed me to believe that Vernon Farmer was a suitable person to select music for an occasion like that? The whole thing was a bit of a farce. Supposed to be a feedback session later on in the afternoon to find out what people thought of it. What fun that is going to be – not. Let's just say I shan't be doing anything similar again in a hurry.

Workshops, seminars and any other activities at two-thirty. Gerald was due to do an hour on 'How to lighten up with the Bible', someone else was leading a walk, a man called Reg Dinsley was supposed to be organising a pool tournament and I, very apprehensively, was about to begin my workshop on 'Fresh Expressions in the Church'.

All but two of the eight people in my workshop looked as if they were hanging about waiting for teatime or the Second Coming, or anything really other than a truly fresh expression. Five from Gerald's church, one being Mirabel Vasey and another Alvin Dekkle, and two from mine, plus Cameron and me. Rather dismayed by Cameron and

Mirabel turning up in the same group. Mirabel's world view is a red – or rather green – rag to a bull as far as Cameron is concerned, and she doesn't seem to be interested in anything but Green issues.

My problem was that, as I'd said to Anne, apart from the fruits of my proogling, I hadn't much idea about the actual meaning of the phrase we were supposed to be discussing, so I really was relying on input from other people. Began by explaining that, as far as I understood (and had read in the course of my internet exploration, although I didn't actually say that, of course) a fresh expression is a form of church for our changing culture, established mainly for people who aren't yet members of any church, and that it could be something completely new and different. Sounded rather good, I thought. Asked the group what they felt about that.

Short, ghastly, strangled silence and seriously absorbed studying of fingernails, then, apropos of nothing, Mirabel said:

'Jesus must have been a piscatorian.'

Sheridan Salmons, a tall, straight-backed, very dignified man in his mid-eighties, murmured, 'Not Church of England, then?'

Mirabel ignored him and explained that a piscatorian is someone who eats fish, but not meat, and if we are trying to be like Jesus, surely none of us should eat meat either.

Cameron, with a very straight face, said, 'When you think about it, Mirabel, why don't we go the whole hog – sorry, I mean go the whole quorn – and have a vegetarian Bible. I mean, Noah's sons, Shem, Ham and Japheth could be renamed Shem, Tofu and Japheth, and Elijah could have a load of nut cutlets dropped on him by ravens when he's hiding by the brook Cherith. Then,' he continued, apparently really fired up, 'you could go through the whole of the Old Testament changing all the burnt offerings into nut cutlets and soya, and when God says in Exodus that the starving Israelites will have meat coming out of their nostrils, it can actually be vegetable mince. What do you think, Mirabel?'

Mirabel said tartly, 'You are thoroughly akin to your political namesake, aren't you, Cameron, speaking as you do through the . . .'

Did my best to drag us back to the point.

'Look, I don't think any of that has got much to do with what we think about Fresh Expressions, has it? We've only got a short time. Let's not waste it.'

Cameron said, 'Sorry, Granddad. Mirabel, you're probably right. I agree that we ought to look at what Jesus did and try to be just like him. Tell you what, maybe we should look at that passage in the eleventh chapter of Mark, the bit where Jesus curses the fig tree and it withers and dies. Now that's leadership by example. Jolly useful, too. If we need a patch of garden cleared we could just stand there and have a good old swear at the plants. Brilliant!'

Aware that Mirabel was about to boil over like a pan of milk, I put my foot down.

'No! No more silliness. We stick to the subject or we don't say anything.'

Couldn't believe that was me speaking, but it certainly did create a brief, simmering silence. Eventually, Duncan Whitton, a dapper little man with soft grey hair and a red bow tie, cleared his throat and said, in his quiet cultured voice, 'Forgive my ignorance, but what exactly is it that we are hoping to freshly express?'

What a relief.

I said, 'Aaah, *good* question, Duncan! *Good, good* question. What does everybody think?'

Alvin Dekkle uncoiled his body from the back of his armchair and responded almost immediately. I've realised who he reminds me of now. There's a bloke on the *Eggheads* quiz I rather like watching on BBC2 who blinks and gasps and pulls faces when someone else gets an answer wrong.

He said, waving his arms in the air as he spoke, 'That's so *typical*!'

Shook his head rapidly from side to side, and made a noise with his mouth like a small motorbike failing to start.

'Wrap it up in words! Make it into a religion. Fill it full of rules. Kill it before it's born. Suck the blood out of it before it has a chance to grow and find an authentic shape. Let's just settle back into tired old middle-class mutual reassurance and forget that there's a real world out there full of people who need somebody who won't pontificate and prattle about concepts that are meaningless to everyone except a handful of people who couldn't give a damn about anyone except themselves. It makes me *sick*! You ask what we're hoping to freshly express? Just *asking* that question makes it pretty well impossible to answer. Don't you see that? You've – you've stamped on it! Do you *really* not see that? Surely you can all see that!'

Fell limply back in his chair as though exhausted by a world capable of displaying such malicious idiocy.

Puzzled pause, then Duncan Whitton said mildly, 'Mmm, right. Sorry, Mr Dekkle. I just wondered – you know – what it's all about. I mean – how are we to do it if we're not allowed to talk about what it is?'

Heavy, intolerably burdened sigh from Dekkle. Hoisted himself wearily forward again and started chopping at the air with both hands, presumably dividing the universe into tidily comprehensible slices for his obtuse listeners.

'Look, I know a man who's been in prison four or five times for the most violent crimes you can imagine. For some reason, I don't know why,' he shrugged modestly, 'I'm the only person he speaks to . . .'

'In the whole world? That's extraordinary!' interposed Cameron innocently.

'What? No!' Dekkle brushed the interruption aside impatiently. 'No, of course not! I mean I'm the only Christian he'll speak to, probably because I make it a point to never, *ever* preach the gospel to him.'

'Ah, yes, with you there,' murmured Cameron solemnly, 'big mistake often made by evangelists, fresh or otherwise.'

Dekkle cast a brief, suspicious glance at Cameron before continuing.

'This man has beaten up his wife several times, he's a serial adulterer, he's been involved in robberies and assaults and violence against the police, he shows no remorse whatsoever for anything he's done and he's told me he'd like to get all the Christians in the world together and use an AK47 on them until the whole place is a bloodbath. And yet!'

Punched the palm of his left hand rhythmically with his fist as he went on.

'And yet this man is closer to Jesus than anyone else I've ever met, and I'll tell you something else. If you ask me

– never mind repentance or salvation or any of those other stupid, hollow words we chuck around – when this bloke dies he'll go *straight* to the place that we so laughingly call heaven!'

Slapped his thighs loudly and looked around triumphantly.

'Well, well,' said Sheridan dryly. 'Goodness me! Quite a revelation. That certainly is a *very* fresh expression of the gospel message in comparison with what I have always understood it to be. So, if I have grasped what you are saying, Mr Dekkle, we Christians are never to commit the dangerous error of preaching the Christian gospel, we are to make ourselves as deeply unpleasant as possible to everyone we encounter, we massacre as large a proportion of the body of Christ as we can reasonably manage, hopefully every single one, and we discard all the essential elements of Christian teaching that we have so foolishly embraced over the last two thousand years. Then, when we die, we march confidently up to the gates of heaven, where God will meet us with a congratulatory smile, slap us on the back and say, "Well *done*, thou good and faithful servant. Enter into my peace. You are in the Genghis Khan Development. Third mansion on the left. Supper's at six."

'Mr Dekkle, forgive me, but would you not agree that your concept of Christian thought and behaviour strays just a tad from the path of orthodoxy as most of us have erroneously, as you maintain, perceived it?'

Dekkle contorted his body into coils of frustration, wrapped his arms tightly around himself and closed his eyes, presumably to blot out the sight of human beings capable of producing such error-saturated nonsense.

'May I say something?' asked Joy Vernables tentatively.

Joy from our church and she's a dear, but she does tend to take a rather convoluted journey towards the point.

'Yes, of course, Joy,' I said, 'only do bear in mind that we have very limited time, and' (stern glance at Alvin Dekkle) 'we've used up quite a lot of it already.'

'Oh yes, I quite understand that, Adrian, and I'll make my point as quickly as I possibly can. Er, how long would you like me to take? Would two minutes be a little long, or should I stop after three or four minutes and ask you if it's OK to carry on until I've got to the . . .'

'Joy, just say it – just *say* it.'

'Right. But you will tell me if I go on for too long, won't you? Because I'd hate to . . .'

'Look, Joy, start telling us what you want to say as soon as I finish this sentence.'

Pause. Joy leaned forward like a sprinter on the blocks.

'Have you finished your sentence?'

'Yes! Start talking now.'

Honestly! Real-life church makes *The Vicar of Dibley* look like a documentary.

'Now?'

'Yes, Joy! Now! Now!'

'Right. Well, my sister-in-law Ellen took me along – well, she didn't take me, I took her, purely in the transport sense, most of the way, anyway. You see, her car had to go in for repairs and she was going to cancel, but I said, no, we'll go in mine. I'll follow you to the garage.'

'Right? Yes, and where were you going?'

'We were going to a Renault garage on the Radford Road. You turn right on the roundabout next to B&Q just before you get into Radford, but you have to be very careful not to take the second . . .'

'Joy, where did you and your sister-in-law go *after* the garage?'

'Oh, sorry, yes, we went to her church for what they call a Saturday Family Breakfast Service. And, well – it was amazing, really amazing.'

'In what way?'

'It was so normal. Mums and dads and children and lots of food and talking and some songs and quite a bit of mess and, right near the end, a little talk – well, more of a story actually, that the children really listened to, most of them, anyway. It was like real people doing real things. That sounds silly, but it's what struck me at the time. And the thing is, Adrian, Ellen told me that quite a lot of the parents who were there never come to church usually. Lots of their children come to a club they run on Monday evenings, but the mums and dads almost never come to the services when they're invited. But now they do. Once a month. They love this Family Breakfast. Honestly, it was so different. So – so normal.'

Duncan was leaning forward and nodding, his eyes alight with interest.

'Fascinating,' he said in his soft voice, 'and I suppose the answer to my question must be veined, as it were, through the body of that experience.'

'Old hat!' interrupted Alvin Dekkle contemptuously from the depths of his sulk.

'Pith helmet!' responded Cameron, not missing a beat. 'Carry on, Duncan.'

'Well, I was just going to say that Joy's description of this particular form of "fresh expression", if that's what it is,

might offer something of a clue. This church was expressing – well, hospitality, generosity and . . .'

'Breakfast!' supplied Sheridan brightly.

'Absolutely! There is something about *breakfast* that is
so very – convivial, is there not?'

'Especially a free one!' added Norman Fellows, speaking
for the first time, and laughing, then blushing richly as the
possible implication of his enthusiasm occurred to him. 'I
– I don't mean that I would want a free breakfast. I mean
that, you know, others would – you know, appreciate it . . .'

'Well exactly, Norman,' continued Duncan kindly, 'and
although Alvin might have slightly over-expressed his point
of view just now . . .'

Grunt from Dekkle.

'I suspect there is a grain of truth in what he said. There
is little point in proclaiming the love of Christ in the
abstract, as it were, if we are not providing the bacon and
eggs to go with it.'

'Or loaves and fishes,' said Cameron.

'With a vegetarian option of organic wholemeal bread
and wild line-caught fish from sustainable stocks,' contrib-
uted Mirabel.

'But how do you *do* something like that?' asked Norman.
'I mean, there's nothing remotely like that in our church at
the moment. It's hard to picture. How do you get it started?'

'I know exactly how to do it,' said Cameron rather
unexpectedly.

'Tell us, Cameron.'

I was beginning to like Duncan.

'Easy! Get my mum to do it. Well, not necessarily my
mum, but someone – people – *like* my mum. Someone

who loves doing things for other people. Someone who really, really loves kids, and respects them and wants them to have a lot of fun. Someone who's even better at being Jesus for people than she is at talking about him. I loved being a kid and having a mum like that. Still do. That's how you do it. Get someone like my mum. She's amazing.'

My grandson!

Quite a good discussion after that.

She's amazing. Yes, she is. If only it was possible to turn your thoughts off when you want them to stop. She is amazing. Is. Is. Is.

When I asked Gerald how his 'Lightening the Bible' session had gone he held his hand flat, outstretched in front of him and rocked it from side to side.

'Good and bad, Dad. Some people loved it. A few radiated unremitting strop vibes from beginning to end.'

'What caused the strop?'

'A couple of things. I started by saying that I agreed one hundred per cent with jolly old Gilbert Chesterton when he said there were three words people really don't want to grapple with: "He became man". God really did become a man. Not a weird man. Not a mutant man. Not a not-really man. True man, as well as being true God. Tempted in exactly the same way as we are.'

'They didn't like that?'

'Well, they kind of went along with it in theory, but there was a distinct whisper of "Burn him!" in the air when I introduced them to my newly discovered Gospel.'

'Your what?'

'My newly discovered Gospel. I found it under a rock in the Middle East last summer. Written in English as well, which simplifies matters.'

'I see. And what is the title of this brand new Gospel written in English?'

Gerald handed me a sheaf of papers.

'Here it is. It's called *The Trivial Gospel According to Fidybus*. I read them three extracts. Two thirds of them nearly wet themselves. The rest controlled their bladders with ease, but weren't so successful with their faces. See what you think. The bits I read are marked with an evil green star.'

I read the extracts.

FIDYBUS 2:16-18

And the Angel Gabriel appeareth unto Simon the fisherman, and he saith unto him, 'Behold I bring thee news of great joy, for thou art to bear a son.'

And immediately Simon fainteth.

When he recovereth the angel saith unto him, 'Fear not, for there is just a chance that I have come to the wrong house . . .'

FIDYBUS 12:16

Later in that same day Jesus picketh an pink flower and sticketh it in his hair. It looketh weird but nice.

FIDYBUS 16:1-3

And again Jesus goeth into the house of Martha and Mary at Bethany, and Martha saith unto him, 'Do you want an egg?'

Jesus replieth, 'Verily I say unto thee I shall not eat another egg until I reach the . . .'

'Do you *want* an *egg*?' Martha interrupteth.

Jesus saith, 'Verily, the sons of perdition shall eat eggs in the age that is to come, but the Son of Man may not . . .'

'*Do* you or do you *not* want an *egg*?'

Jesus replieth, 'What? Oh, yes, two please, lightly boiled – about three minutes – with a few soldiers – I mean, conscientious objectors – made of unleavened bread – can I have the burnt bits scraped off? Thank you. Cheers. Where was I? Oh, yes. Verily I say unto thee – oh, and er plenty of salt, on the side, in a little pile. Magic. No, not magic. I mean – great!'

'What do you think?'

I shook my head helplessly.

'It's wonderful, Gerald, but I suppose some of these tradi-tional types go ballistic at the very idea of putting words into Jesus' mouth, especially when they're flippant ones.'

'Yes, I think you could be right about that, Dad. And I might have made things worse with my next offering.'

'Tell me.'

'Well, Nancy Duphrane – she's the tall, thin, very aristo-cratic lady dressed in expensive autumn colours – she and I were talking a few weeks ago about King Solomon and what a miserable old beggar he must have been, judging by some of the stuff he wrote. So we put together a dialogue between the king and his counsellor. And we read it in the seminar. It's in there with the Fidybus stuff. Have a read later on. One thing I can say – I definitely lightened the

Bible for most of my group. The rest probably want to lock it up so that I can never get my hands on those sacred pages again. Funny old world, isn't it, Dad?'

'Hilarious. Don't give up, though.'

Took Gerald and Daphne's sketch through to read over a cup of tea and a piece of cake.

COUNSELLOR: OK, where do you want to start?

SOLOMON: (*blowing air from expanded cheeks*) This is not easy.

C: I understand. Take your time.

S: (*clears his throat*) I'm here because I need to talk to someone about – something.

C: (*nods encouragingly*) Ri-i-i-ght. That's what I'm here for. Go on.

S: This is, er, confidential, isn't it?

C: Completely confidential. Nothing goes outside this room. Promise.

S: Right, that's good, because if you did tell anyone what I say I'd need to have you torn to pieces by ravenous wild dogs.

C: (*nods acceptingly*) That's fair enough.

S: (*deep breath*) OK. Well, it's about – it's about my concubines.

C: Your concubines.

S: Yes. Apparently there are three hundred of them. Don't know how they managed to get so many together in the same place, but yes, three hundred concubines.

C: You said 'Apparently'. Do you mean you've never actually – you know?

S: Nope! Never seen them, never been near them. Never wanted to. Thing is – I'm supposed to be, you know, wise and powerful and all that – King Solomon! – but I just don't think I'm ever going to be turned on by concubines – not in that way, anyway. I don't see how anyone could. I mean, I'm sure they could make good pets, but . . .

c: Pets?

s: Yes, having *one* around the place wouldn't be so bad, a tame one, as long as it kept its distance. You know, quite novel, but I mean, you wouldn't want to take the chance of getting behind an angry concubine, would you? I gather they fire their thingamabobs backwards at you when they're cross?

SILENCE

c: Your majesty, what do you think a concubine is?

s: What? Same as you, of course. What – you want me to tell you?

c: Yes, if you don't mind.

s: All right. Let me see. Concubine. Well, it's a mammal. Er, lives on insects and that sort of thing – I think. About two foot tall. Long thin nose like a tube. Covered in long spikes. That's about all I know.

SILENCE

c: Have you got any ID on you?

s: No, look, I really am him. I am wise King Solomon. You might not think so, but I am. Why, why? What did I say?

c: Your Majesty, a concubine is a woman. A perfectly normal woman. You've got three hundred attractive women all ready and waiting for you to – you know. I think you might be mixing them up with porcupines.

s: (*hugely surprised and relieved*) Ooooooh, right! Well, that explains it then. I always did wonder why they thought I would get so excited about having three hundred spiny anteaters – I mean it did seem weird. I'm *so* glad to know this, because I was always a bit worried about what I'd do with them if – you know – if I ever got in there. That's why I never went. Every now and then one of my servants would say, 'Your concubines await, Sire.' And I'd say, 'Well, what am I going to do with them?' And they'd say, you know, 'Have your way with them, Your Majesty,' and wink at me and elbow each other in the ribs. And I'd say, 'Well, I don't really think I actually want to, 'cause of all the spines and that. (*after a moment's reflection*) Blimey, I don't know about wise, they must have thought I was completely bonkers!

C: So you think knowing this will help?

s : Oh gosh, yes! Now I can get on with my life. I've been feeling so inadequate and low. You wouldn't believe the depressive rubbish I've been churning out. Oh, my good-ness! For example, my next thing is looking really dark. I've got it here, look. I thought I might call it 'Ecclesiastes'. Good title?

C: Brilliant, your Majesty!

s: You're not just saying that to avoid being torn to pieces by ravenous wild dogs?

C: Good Lord, no. *Brilliant* title!

s: Good, well this is all I've written so far:

> 'Meaningless! Meaningless!'
> Says the teacher.
> 'Utterly meaningless!
> Everything is meaningless,
> When you're expected to spend your time with
>   aggressive, spiky mammals.'

In view of what you've told me I might cut that last bit out. After all, on the bright side, there's plenty more to be miserable about. Chasing after the wind. All things are wearisome. All flesh is grass – that's one of mine. Those are three of the topics I was planning to cover. What do you think?

c: (*sighs*) I think I'd better see you next Tuesday, your Majesty. Untold riches, total power and supernatural wisdom. Oh, and three hundred concubines, remember? (*dryly*) Try to stay positive.

Sometimes I wish I was Gerald. Occasionally I'm really quite glad I'm not.

Slightly dismayed to find that Minnie Stamp was sitting next to me in the planning meeting after tea for tomorrow's Communion service, so I decided to ask for her ideas first and get it over with. Worked hard yet again at sounding neutral and quietly confident and content, but without much hope.

'OK, Minnie, let's start with you. Any ideas?'

Stroked my arm with one limp flipper and reacted as though I'd collapsed in a neurotic heap.

'Look, it's all going to work out, Adrian, honestly. Cross my heart and hope to die, and hope even more to *rise* again.'

She emitted a trickling laugh and glanced around, presumably seeking appreciation of her 'spiritual' jest.

'We'll all support you. All of us are Adrian-friends, aren't we, everybody? Let's all give Adrian a little clap to show that we value him.'

Oh, *no*!

Embarrassed smattering of applause from the co-opted 'Adrian-friends'. Controlled myself with an effort. Acknowledged the encouragement with a Queen Elizabeth-like wave.

'Good! OK. Thanks. What's your idea, Minnie?'

'Right, said Minnie, patting her bony little knees excitedly. 'I've got something really super and smashing and spiritual to suggest. What we do is – we get some paper and we cut it into leaf shapes, and we paint them all green. Or we could get some green paper and cut it into leaf shapes, which would, you know, save the trouble of painting each leaf individually. And then we take the green leaf shapes and on each one we write the name of someone we really loathe. You know, someone we loathe, but we don't want to loathe. None of us want to loathe, do we? We want to lovey-dove them, like we all lovey-dove Adrian. We don't want to loathe them.'

'You'll be first on my leaf,' I thought. Didn't say it, of course.

'And when we've got all the leaves with names of people we loathe on them we stick them to a sort of tree during the service, and that becomes our loathing tree. A tree covered in people we loathe. And then we burn the tree, we burn the people we loathe. Actually, we don't burn the people we loathe. That would be wrong. We burn the leaves with their names on, so we sort of burn the loathing. We burn the loathing up until it's a-a-a-all gone! You see, when we've burned the loathing tree, all the loathing's gone because – because we've burned it. It's very, very spiritual and – and very spiritual. It's really worked well for me in the past. In fact, I have real trouble thinking of anyone to write down on my leaf when I do it nowadays because – you know, so much of the loathing's gone. Burned away.'

Breathy giggle.

Short, depressed silence.

Eventually Dennis raised himself from his floating lilo on one elbow and said, 'Minnie, thanks very much for that. I don't know what Adrian thinks, but I reckon we should save that idea for when we're back in our own churches and, you know, people feel safer because they all know each other. What do you think?'

Minnie pushed her head forward like a myopic tortoise and looked at me with a ludicrously exaggerated expression of respectful submission.

She said, 'I think we have to remember that *Adrian's* in charge of planning the service, aren't you, Adrian?

'Er, yes, yes . . .'

'And we all respect you.'

She waved her finger to and fro in front of her face like a small windscreen wiper.

'And *you*,' the latter word had at least three syllables, and her tone was coaxing and roguish, '*you* have to jolly well learn to respect yourself.'

She called in the troops again.

'Doesn't he, Adrian-friends?'

Saved from committing murder by Josey suddenly releasing an explosion of laughter that somehow forced its way out through her nose, so that she had to be rescued with tissues pinched from one of the prayer stations. Anyway, Minnie's dreadful idea got shelved, so that was all right.

One very good suggestion from Donald Fitley. Said he'd heard Father John speak somewhere in the past, and it was brilliant.

'It might be too late to ask,' he said, 'but why not use him while he's here? We haven't got anyone for the morning slot on Sunday. How about asking Father John if he'd mind doing a half-hour question and answer session after breakfast, then a short preach in the Communion service?'

Dennis removed his Ray-Ban shades and regained consciousness for long enough to say that he was more than happy to step aside if Father John was OK to do it, especially as he hadn't prepared anything yet, and I said I thought it was a fantastic idea as long as Father John didn't mind. All the Adrian-friends agreed, without feeling the need to applaud.

All came together pretty well after that.

Found Father John and asked him how he would feel about doing the morning session and the sermon at such short notice.

'Answering questions is fine,' he replied. 'I can bore for England as long as people keep firing stuff at me. I'll do my very best, but only if I'm allowed to ask all of you a question as well. Agreed?'

'Agreed.'

Suddenly found myself really looking forward to this session. Father John never seems to go in the direction you expect. Gets a bit disconcerting at times, but, as Anne says, there's so much love about when he talks.

'And I think a little talk should be OK. The theme?'

'Same as the weekend – "Where is the Love?" Anything you like, really. I know it's stupidly late to ask, but I'm sure the Holy Spirit will give you something to say.'

Father John chuckled.

'The Holy Spirit? Or adrenalin? Although adrenalin was invented by God, of course. Hmm. That talk I did at Devizes in 1957 that went down so well? The old reliable mix of fear and vanity? Something will come along, Adrian. Thank you. Yes, I will do that for you.'

Excellent!

Feedback session at a quarter to six with all the members of both churches to find out what people thought of the silent meal. Dreading it.

Several comments about the strange nature of the music. Not very surprising really. How could Vernon Farmer have been obtuse enough to suppose that 'The Dambusters March' played at ear-shattering volume could be construed as inspiring and godly music? When I rushed over (silently) and hissed at him to change it for something more peaceful and spiritual he played two gloomy Leonard Cohen tracks, followed by a dark, droning Bob Dylan song that began:

> Congratulations, for breaking my heart,
> Congratulations, for tearing me apart . . .

Duncan Whitton mentioned this and said politely but firmly that he'd never have sat down to eat if he'd known there was going to be music to hang yourself by.

Vernon said that it wasn't his fault, because he'd looked at the title and thought it was a Cliff Richard track.

Mrs Duphrane said she was glad it hadn't been because it was difficult to eat and vomit at the same time, especially in silence.

Outraged protestations from several offended Cliff Richard fans in our church, one of whom said that in her opinion Cliff Richard was not only the best Christian singer in the entire world, but the best singer of any kind in the entire history of music.

Mrs Duphrane said that, in that case, every other Christian singer in the entire world must have died or been transported to heaven, and wasn't it a relief to learn that God had such good taste in choosing who he wanted to hang out with.

Uproar. When it was finally quelled, asked if there were any more useful observations on musical aspects of the silent meal. Only other comment was from Cameron, who suggested that it would have made all the difference if I'd brought along my beautiful recording of the Sex Pistols singing 'Kum Ba Yah'. Stupid boy!

Rather negative contribution from Mrs Struthers, an elderly lady who looks very much like those old pictures of Billy Bunter's sister, Bessie, about a table of children who, she sourly complained, had managed to create mayhem in exactly the normal way but without actually speaking.

Some truth in this. At one point I had myself seen Eamonn Cluskey grind his younger brother Patrick's face into half a plateful of shepherd's pie with concentrated energy, and then, when his victim emerged spluttering and enraged, hold his finger to his lips with urgent, faked concern and genuinely wicked relish to indicate that speaking was not allowed. Polly Cluskey, their mother, then threw her napkin down on the table where she was sitting, got to her feet with a great scraping of chair feet against the stone-tiled floor, and marched across the dining hall with tightly compressed lips to undertake the problematic task of miming silently but furiously that, if they didn't 'behave', both brothers would go straight to bed after supper.

Gasping with shocked outrage, Patrick jabbed his blunt dagger of a finger into the chest of his smugly smiling older brother, vigorously but soundlessly mouthing the injustice of it all. Poor Polly stood for a few moments, head forward, hands on hips, trying to convey through the sheer quivering rigidity of her body, that, whoever had started it, it had better stop now! As soon as she turned away Eamonn grabbed his brother's prodding, accusative finger, forcibly inserted the offending digit into a cheese and pickle filled bread roll, and dunked the whole thing in a jug of water.

It occurred to me that it would most likely be Polly who went to bed early in the end.

Did we not consider, Mrs Struthers wanted to know, that keeping to the letter of the law was of little use if the substance of a rule was to be ignored?

Rather surprisingly, Father John said that he agreed, and went on to say that it was a bit like forgiveness.

'Every Sunday,' he explained, 'we say some words kindly given to us by Jesus as an example of how we might pray, and one line in that prayer asks God to forgive us only to the extent that we forgive others. Well, there's not a lot of point in parroting those words each week if have no intention of doing anything about it, is there? Suppose, for instance that this lady – what is your first name, my dear sister?'

There was a pause while (as Gerald put it later) Mrs Struthers dug her Christian name out of the dusty old trunk in which it had been stored.

'My, er, my first name is Enid,' she replied, her eyes opening a little wider than usual.

'Yes, well, suppose that you, Enid, instead of extending love and understanding to parents like Polly, who honestly and truly do their very best to be good mums and dads, were to take a hard and unforgiving view, and make them feel even worse than they do already. Just imagine that! It would hardly be worthwhile to say that prayer on a Sunday, would it? No, no, thank you so much for making the point. The law is just a scaffold for love, isn't it? And when, one day, we have finished building our house of love, God will whisk away the scaffolding and the house will stand up all on its own. Thank you, Enid.'

Mrs Struthers subsided, looking a little dazed.

Huge Mrs Danby-Carstairs from Gerald's church rose majestically to her feet, pointed dramatically at tiny Mr Fitley from our church and accused him of catching her eye during the meal and making suggestive movements with his head in the direction of a clump of bushes just outside the dining-room window. Mr Fitley, with shock, abject terror and profound indignation struggling for first position in his expression, denied the accusation with desperate, stammering passion. He said that he had only been asking for the salt to be passed, and hadn't been sure how to do it when you weren't allowed to speak.

Mrs Danby-Carstairs lowered herself slowly back onto her long-suffering chair, momentarily becalmed, but clearly advertising her readiness to be whipped into a froth by any further storms of offence.

Norman Fellows, who had been sitting on the same table as Mrs Danby-Carstairs, suddenly became agitated and said that he owed Mr Fitley an apology for his unspoken interpretation of what he now realised was a mime indicating the use of a salt cellar, that had accompanied the head movements objected to by Mrs Danby-Carstairs.

Asked Norman what he was talking about.

He turned bright scarlet and refused to say any more.

Honestly! No wonder the comments tended to be negative. Not quite the eloquent meeting of the eyes that Denver Doesn't-know-what-he's-talking-about-shouldn't-write-any-more-nonsense Mountainberger rambled on about in his blasted book. Why do these amazing spiritual experiences always happen to someone else?

It strongly reminded me of Let God Spring into Royal Acts of Harvest Growth, the big Christian festival that used to happen down at Wetbridge, the place where our tent got blown away by the wind. Everyone else would come back from their seminars filled with excitement and say things like, 'Wow! You should have been there, you absolutely should! God really *moved* in a mighty way among his people! So many healings and manifestations and fantastic prophesies and people being slain in the Spirit and – and wow! You should have been there!'

'That's nice,' we would reply feebly, 'we had a great time too. We went to a very nice talk about the reorganisation of hierarchical structures in post-evangelical urban Anglicanism. Lots of – you know – flow charts and black marker pens and great things like that.'

'And did God, you know, really *move* among his people?'

'Erm, well, on this particular occasion his people were perhaps not the liveliest bunch, all very busy taking notes and things, but yes, I'm sure he must have done a little bit of, er, moving . . .'

On these occasions Anne always used to say, 'Yes, but here's the question. Was God excluding or protecting us?' Gerald would laugh at this, and so would I, despite not knowing what she meant.

Last time I get involved with a silent meal. Dambusters! I ask you . . .

Had a few quiet moments with Anne after the feedback meeting. Asked her if she ever felt that Mrs Duphrane was deliberately provocative. Threw her head back and laughed like a drain.

Why?

Asked her what made my question so hilariously amusing.

She said, 'I love her – so funny. But she's lonely, sweetheart, and bored. Everyone needs a hobby, don't they?'

Do they? Pretended to know what she was talking about.

7

Saturday Evening

Karina collected used dishes from the table next to ours at the end of dinner this evening. When she saw me she smiled and waved wildly, flapping her arms like a giant bird and calling out, 'Look at me – I fry like a bustard!'

Gerald and Cameron glanced at each other, then leaned towards me enquiringly.

Said nothing.

Cameron said, 'Granddad, we're going to get some coffee and sit comfortably in the Lounge so that we can really concentrate on you telling us why a Latvian girl would randomly flap her arms at you and say she was frying like a bustard.'

Really didn't have the energy to even try to explain. I know better. Anne can tell them. She'll enjoy that.

Call from Leonard just after dinner to say Angels has fallen out big-time with the lady in the SatNav and refuses to be in the same car with her, especially after the 'field incident'. Apparently, Angels is complaining that the tone used by 'Katy' has become more and more bossy and sarcastic as the journey has gone on, and she's not putting up with it any more. Yesterday, after Katy had ordered 'Take the exit' for the third time, and just before Leonard began his fourth circuit of the Scotch Corner roundabout, Angels shouted,

'We've all been through PMT in our time, sweetheart, but you're supposed to be a professional!'

Tried to point out that 'Katy' is just a computer-generated voice, but Leonard said, 'Yes, I know, but, to be fair, Adrian, lots of people are computer-generated, and I wish they could have had the same start in life as us. I know that's not their fault, but it's no excuse for getting more and more bad-tempered, is it?'

Someone ought to run day-trips to Planet Thynn.

Also asked him why they were at Scotch Corner when they should have been a hundred miles further south, but got cut off at that moment. Just have to wait for him to get in touch later I suppose.

Very short but deeply alarming text from Leonard shortly before the evening entertainment was due to start, asking, 'in case it became necessary to know', if I could tell him which side of the road they drive on in Holland. That'll be Katy getting her own back I expect. (What am I saying? It's always a seriously bad sign when I find myself entering too far into Thynn's strange world.) Will we ever see them again? Anyone's guess.

Entertainment was due to begin at eight o'clock. I always dread these ghastly things when they happen during church weekends where I'm a speaker. They go on for about three days, and enjoying any aspect of them depends almost entirely on knowing exactly why it's so excruciatingly funny for everyone when dear old whiskery George comes up the front wearing a Second World War gas mask and announces that he's moving to Croydon next Friday. Actually, scratch that, it's probably not much funnier when you do know.

One point I made very strongly to Richard earlier in the day was that he mustn't let parents bully him into letting their children play musical instruments in the entertainment if they hadn't put their names down on the list by mid-afternoon, and he must make sure they weren't all planning to play the same piece of music.

'If', I said sternly, 'we have the same ghastly tune inflicted on us more than twice at the very most, I shall hold you personally responsible, and probably despatch you to heaven before midnight strikes. Do I make myself clear?'

'Oh, yes, of course,' said Richard. 'I – I shall certainly do my best.'

'They'll come up to you just before it begins,' I warned darkly. 'People who have always seemed reasonable and pleasant and Christian in the past, and they'll plead and coax and bribe and threaten you into letting them add "just one more teensy-weensy item to the programme". And you will say – what, Richard? What will you say?'

'Er, I shall say, "Well, it's very kind of you to offer, but . . ."'

'No, you won't say that, Richard, because if you do they'll just steam-roller you and do what they like. What you need to say is, "No! Absolutely not! It's too late." Clear?'

'Er, clear. Yes, yes, quite clear.'

Just before the entertainment began I whispered to Richard as he stood nervously at the back of the Hexagonal Lounge, 'Everything OK?'

'Yes, yes, fine, Adrian. All ready to go, I think.'

'No extra items?'

'No – well, just two or three little additions. Very, very little ones. Tiny, tiny ones.'

'Hmm . . .'

Felt quite tense when Cameron went up soon after the beginning of the entertainment to do his quiz. Felt a lot better when he announced that the first question was about a well-known Christian book. Told myself nothing could go too far wrong with subjects like Christian literature.

Cameron asked Sheridan Salmons to come up to the front and face the audience.

'Now,' said Cameron, 'in a moment, Mr Salmons, you'll hear a noise behind you, and you have to guess which famous Christian book it represents.'

Noticed Joy Venables creeping up the side of the hall, holding a blown-up brown paper bag. She burst it just behind Mr Salmon's ear with the most almighty BANG! I think he might have actually left the floor before landing and turning to see what was going on behind him.

'Ah!' he said, revolving back towards the audience with a delighted smile on his face, his dignity apparently intact. *Surprised by Joy*. A Lewis classic. Very good, my boy.'

Tumultuous applause. I thought Cameron was lucky not to get his head smacked. How on earth did he persuade Joy to do something like that? Like father, like son, presumably.

Hardly dared watch my grandson's next offering.

He called three ladies out to line up at the front. Must have been in on whatever was going on, judging by their giggles. I know two of them well. They're older ladies who've lost their husbands in the last few years, and get together most weeks for coffee or lunch. The other one was from Gerald's church – Mrs Duphrane, the tall, posh-looking lady who asked Alan Varney that straight-faced question yesterday evening.

'Right,' said Cameron, 'I'm going to ask each of these beautiful ladies a question, and you all have to guess which story about Jesus we're illustrating. Here goes!' He glanced at his clipboard. 'Now, Mrs Watson, you're first. Here's my question for you. Do you think you would?'

Little, robin-like Mrs Watson chirruped coyly, 'Well, it's possible, yes.'

'OK, good, and Mrs Duphrane, are you likely to?'

Mrs Duphrane appeared to give the question grave consideration.

'Yes!' she said firmly at last, in her posh, hoarse voice, 'given the appropriate circumstances I would most definitely be tempted.'

'Excellent. And finally, Mrs Osbourne, you likely to have a go?'

Betty Osbourne is a good friend of mine. Lovely daughter called Poppy who works away up north somewhere. Betty has the sad charm of a basset hound, and is an expert at making me laugh when I've decided I won't. She scanned the audience with her wide, kind, mournful eyes for a moment as if seeking inspiration, and said, 'Ooooh no, I wouldn't rule it out at all, not at all, not *yet* anyway. Depends of course . . .'

'There we are, then,' said Cameron brightly, addressing the rows of puzzled faces. 'Any ideas? A famous story about Jesus.'

Slightly uneasy silence. Half of those present must have been wondering if these obscurely vulgar pieces of dialogue were pushing the boundaries of 'Christian fun' a little too far. Some just looked puzzled.

'Shall I put them out of their misery?' enquired Mrs Duphrane archly.

'Yes,' said Cameron, 'go ahead.'

'It's The Widow's Mite. Come on, keep up! The widow's mite – the widows *might*. Got it, sweet things?'

The 'sweet things' certainly got it, though some of them clearly didn't really want it. Mrs Duphrane made things worse as she returned to her seat by muttering audibly and expensively, 'Chance'd be a fine thing.'

Gerald didn't help either at this point by choking with laughter.

Oh dear. It's in the genes I suppose.

Next time someone else can be in charge of the joke bit of the entertainment. All a bit nerve-racking when you don't know what the jokes are in advance. Trouble is, one man's hilarious joke is another man's cause for deep offence. And you never know with Christians. Sometimes they laugh uproariously at things that seem way over the mark, other times they go all stony-faced and disapproving over nothing at all.

There's a plump, red-cheeked, middle-aged man in Gerald's church called Reg Dinsley. He organised a pool tournament earlier in the day. I've met him before on a couple of occasions. Reminds me a bit of Anne's Uncle Ralph, now departed this life to whichever section of eternity is best suited to jokes about suppositories and dogs who've eaten condoms, to name just a couple of his favourite themes. There were times when Uncle Ralph made Roy Chubby Brown look like Mother Teresa.

Rather dismayed when Dinsley came rolling up to the front as soon as I asked if anyone had got any jokes.

I said, 'Keep 'em clean, eh, Reg!' in what was supposed to be a jovial, roguish Christian sort of voice. Came out a bit high-pitched and strangled.

'OK,' said Dinsley, 'here's one to start you off! Did you hear about the happy lorry driver? He was HGV positive! Ha-ha-ha-ha!'

Tried to make noises that combined mild amusement, grown-up disapproval, a hope that people would tolerate Reg Dinsley in order that he might be drawn into the kingdom, and cheery assertion that this was the last joke of its kind that we would be hearing this evening. Didn't quite work. Gerald said afterwards that he was so fascinated by the words and noises coming out of my mouth that he wrote them down. He showed me.

'Chah! Hmm . . . Well! I don't – aaaah . . . So. OK. Ri-i-i-i-ght! Erm . . .'

Good of him to take the trouble.

Next one wasn't much better. A very, very long joke told by an enormously fat man who was a day visitor to Scarleeswanvale and wasn't supposed to be in our thing anyway. The joke ended with the man doing a horribly vigorous mime of chewing a toffee in his bottom. I already deal regularly with a little clutch of ghastly images that I can't get out of my mind. I didn't need a new one.

Gerald offered some thoughts on Christians involved in sport.

'Tennis players,' he announced with ominous confidence, 'make very bad Christians. Why? Because, to them, love means nothing.'

Groans from all present.

He also volunteered information about identifying the churchmanship of rugby teams.

'For instance,' he explained, 'you can always tell when a rugby team's *not* Anglican, because the front row is fully occupied, the scrum sings "Bind us Together" when they pack down, hookers are welcome, they are perfectly happy about going from three points to five, and they've worked out how to do conversions. Simple!'

Tricky moment later on when a little girl called Sadie came up and said with sweetly unaffected pride, 'I done a annamagram of the ladies who take us with Anne in the mornings. For Sarah an' Megan. Can I tell them to everyone?'

Glanced up and noticed the faces of the two Angels of Death like pallid moons in the half-light at the back of the meeting room.

I said, a little uneasily, 'Aaah, that's – lovely! So, you've done a . . .'

'Annamagram.'

'An an-a-gram,' I corrected in suitably avuncular, lightly instructive fashion.

'Yes, a am-a-gram for Sarah and Megan.'

'Good, off you go then. We all want to hear them. We all want to hear them, don't we everybody?'

Murmurs of encouragement from the audience.

'You want to hear them, don't you, Sarah and Megan?'

Sarah and Megan radiated menace and curses from their pit of doom at the back. Rest of the audience continued to oblige with the usual nods and vocal cow impressions.

'Mmm! Mmm! Mmm!'

Sadie glanced at a scrap of paper in her hand, then looked up and spoke brightly and boldly:

'Here they are. Sarah is a amagram of "a rash", and Megan is a amagram of "mange".

Paralysed moment followed by a round of troubled applause. Very conscious of Uncle Fester's nieces glaring with frozen malevolence from the shadows that seemed to swirl around the back row of the audience. Thank goodness for Anne. How in the name of Beelzebub did we end up with these terrifying women?

Skinny, nineteen-year-old Adam Baxter from our church is a wildly enthusiastic new convert. Came up to the front and announced excitedly that he'd spent half the night writing a Christian 'Rap', more or less at the direct dictation of the Holy Spirit.

Why does my heart sink like a stone when I hear people say things like that?

'Thing is,' said Adam breathlessly, 'we people in the Church ought to be able to do Rap and stuff just as well as non-Christian rappers like the one who's named after the coloured chocolate button things.'

Audience exchanged mystified glances.

'I think he means Eminem,' groaned Gerald, who was holding his hands over his head as though something dreadfully heavy was about to fall on him.

Adam's performance did seem rather strange to me. Maybe it's because I don't understand Rap. Did some weird things with his hands, passing them to and fro in front of his face while doing what looked, inexplicably, like the Wolf

Cub Scout sign with his fingers. Very odd. Also, as the Rap
went on he sounded more and more like Frank Spencer in
the venerable TV show *Some Mothers Do 'Ave 'Em*. Got a
copy of the words from him afterwards.

I wake up in the morning and I pra-a-a-ay,
Every da-a-a-ay
Even when it's gre-e-e-ey
It makes me feel oka-a-a-ay
In every wa-a-a-ay
When I pra-a-a-ay
I like to write my prayers down when I pra-a-a-ay
I write on strips of paper and I put them in a
      tra-a-a-ay
I've got a name for the tra-a-a-ay
It's called a pra-a-a-ay tra-a-a-ay
My prayers are always answered
Sometimes with a yea-a-a-ah
And sometimes with a na-a-a-ay
Sometimes with a wa-a-a-
-it
But he-e-e-ey
I am always grea-a-a
-tful
So whether you are clergy or whether you are
      la-a-a-ay
Do *not*, do *not*, do *not*, do *not* neglect
To pra-a-a-ay
No wa-a-a-ay
Oka-a-a-ay
I'm not ga-a-a-ay

I used to have a girlfriend called Fa-a-a-ay
To protect the girl I've had to change her na-a-a-
-me
That's all I have to sa-a-a-ay
Toda-a-a-ay
Spects!

Spects? Does that *mean* something?

As the entertainment ground mercilessly on, I discovered what Richard's 'two or three little additions' were. Honestly! Why do I bother saying anything to anybody about anything? Poor old Richard was obviously mown down like a solitary stalk of wheat in the path of a combine harvester. The power of the proud parent is awesome and virtually irresistible.

Item six: five-year-old Kitty Burlesford playing 'Twinkle, Twinkle Little Star' on the violin.

Item seven: six-year-old George Farmer Junior playing 'Twinkle, Twinkle Little Star' on the violin.

Item ten: Patrick Cluskey playing 'Twinkle, Twinkle Little Star' on the violin.

Item thirteen: five-year-old Nancy Calthrop playing 'Twinkle, Twinkle Little Star' on the violin.

Unbelievable!

To cap it all off, and just as it seemed possible that the agony might be over and the long-term healing about to begin, Dennis Strang chose this very moment to bestir himself from his beachside deckchair to suggest that 'the lovely children' join together for one final rendition . . . cue the dubious delights of Kitty Burlesford *and* George Farmer Junior *and* Patrick Cluskey *and* Nancy Calthrop playing

'Twinkle, Twinkle Little Star' together – or to be strictly accurate, not together – two or three times over. It sounded like a metaphor for the groaning, whining, cataclysmic collapse of some once-great civilisation. Felt at the end as if I'd woken up from major surgery only to be told that it had been unsuccessful.

Gerald leaned across as they finished to suggest that we find the man who wrote 'Twinkle, Twinkle Little Star', and ask if he didn't think there was enough wrong with the world without this ghastly musical fungus that seems to grow like mould over all church weekend entertainments. Nodded agreement – and applauded wildly at the same time like all the rest. No choice. You have to, don't you?

I knew Cameron had written a song especially for the entertainment. What I didn't realise was that his inspiration for this major piece of work was one of my 'trivial obsessions' as Anne and Gerald annoyingly call them.

'Right, now I'm going to do a song for you, and it's based on one of the things that my granddad goes on and on about, at least according to Grandma and my dad. They told me that whenever there's a choice of jobs to be done in the house he always chooses the hoovering, because it's one of the things he actually understands how to do.'

Cheek!

'But apparently he gets very peevish and grumpy when the tool you do the edges with is missing. Dad says you quite often hear him calling out from some remote corner of the house like a lost soul: "The crevice tool! Where's the crevice tool? The crevice tool's not in its slot! Who's not put the crevice tool away in its slot? It's not in its allocated slot. Honestly! Other people!"'

Cameron's impression of me calling out in a high-pitched querulous voice like a deranged octogenarian was completely inaccurate, but at least it made people laugh. Gritted my teeth and waited for it all to finish.

'Once,' continued Cameron, 'he got so obsessed with the whole floor-cleaning thing, that he actually thought he *was* a hoover. Went berserk. In fact, it got so bad that in the end . . .' His tone became grave to the point of tragedy. 'We called the police, and he had to be suctioned.'

'Get on with the song!'

At least I got a bit of a laugh as well.

'Anyway,' said Cameron, 'I've written this song to celebrate the crevice tool that Granddad loves so much. I'm going to sing it, and Adam's going to help me with a few little mimes as we go along.'

Cameron sang with a pseudo-operatic voice, rather in the style of George Dawes, the character played by Matt Lucas in the old TV quiz show *Shooting Stars*. I must say Adam seemed much happier and more sane messing about during the verses and duelling against Cameron with the two crevice tools they'd somehow managed to find. Hope they put them carefully back in the slots they came from . . .

These were the words of the song.

The crevice tool, the crevice tool,
It's very, very useful and it's very, very cool,
You learn how to use it at the crevice tool school,
Ho! for the crevice tool.

The crevice tool, the crevice tool,
The very thought of using it is making me drool,
I think I may be standing in a little drool pool,
Fruit! of the crevice tool.

The crevice tool, the crevice tool,
If you get a couple you can use them for a duel,
Whether you're from Hartlepool or Liverpool, you'll,
Fight! with the crevice tool.

The crevice tool, the crevice tool,
Very good defence against an ogre or a ghoul,
Banning it from use would be a very cruel rule,
Stand! For the crevice tool.

The crevice tool, the crevice tool,
Give it to your cousin in the season of Yule,
If he doesn't like it he's a crevice tool fool,
Sing! Of the crevice tool.

Oh, si-i-i-ng of the cre-e-evice too-o-ol!
The crevice tool.

Most surprising contribution from little Donald Fitley, who announced that he was a life-long Bob Dylan fan, and had written his own version of a well-known Dylan song that he would like to sing for us. A silence, compounded of shock and slight concern, fell over the audience as they waited. This turned to tumultuous applause after Donald sang the following words in a voice remarkably close to the familiar gravelly tones.

Come chemists and drugstores throughout the mall,
Those throat sweets you sold me are no good at all,
My temperature's risen as high as Nepal,
A severe influenza is lurking,
And I sound like a shovel being scraped down a wall,
For the Strepsils, they are not working.

I only got the one verse down, but it made quite an impact.

Josey raised her hand towards the end of the entertainment and asked if it would be all right to read a little poem that she'd written a few days earlier. Stood at the front looking a bit nervous.

'I never write poetry, and this isn't really poetry.'

She did a sort of throwing away movement with the sheet of paper she was holding in one hand.

'I'm sure it's no good – it's just a sort of rhyming thing. But – but I thought you might like to hear it.'

Encouraging murmurs.

'I met this little girl, you see, and you know how children tell you about their lives as though there's nothing more important in the whole world. Well, she wanted me to know that her hamster had died a few days before. Apparently its teeth got very long and were going bad, and the little girl's mummy and daddy said they would have to take him to the vet. So they put him in a cardboard box and he just sat there without moving all the way to the surgery. And when they got there the vet looked at the hamster and said that it was very poorly and should be put to sleep. Afterwards they took the little body home in its box and had a burial service in the garden. It was very, very sad, the little girl said, and would I write a poem about it for her? I'd never written anything like that before, but she was so earnest and I was so surprised that I said yes. I asked what her hamster was called, hoping that it might be something easy to find rhymes for. When she said he was called Fudge I got a bit worried. But I did my best. I'll read it to you.

Cleaning you and feeding you, it never was a drudge,
Dear Fudge.
Your teeth got long and bad, and God gave us a
     nudge,
'Help Fudge.'
We put you in a cardboard box, you didn't even
     budge,
Poor Fudge.
We gave you to the vet, but you never bore a grudge,
Sweet Fudge.
We dug a little hole and we buried you in sludge,
Oh, Fudge.
We stood beside your grave, it was a little muddy
     smudge,
No Fudge.
Leaving you was horrible, a slow, unhappy trudge,
Bye, Fudge.
Hamster hell or heaven? Who are we to judge?
Our Fudge?'

Josey got a laugh for each one of her rhymes, and an actual round of highly deserved applause when she got to 'sludge'.
   Wonderful and totally unexpected end to the entertainment. Richard announced that a very talented violinist was

coming up to finish the evening for us. To a round of applause, my bird-impersonating friend Karina came demurely to the front holding a violin and bow. Placing the instrument beneath her chin with classical expertise she proceeded to play 'Twinkle, Twinkle, Little Star' extremely badly.

Couldn't believe it! What on earth was Richard thinking of? Slightly puzzled applause as Karina finished her screeching journey to the end of the tune, then Richard stepped forward once more.

'Karina might not be very good at the moment,' he said, 'but I know that she is planning to improve. In fact, in just a little while, she's hoping to be – *this* good.'

He waved the Latvian girl forward. Her second rendering of 'Twinkle, Twinkle' was a huge improvement on the first. Tumultuous applause this time. We'd caught on.

'And in a few years,' continued Richard, brimming with new-found confidence, 'her ambition is to be *this* good!'

This time it was 'Twinkle, Twinkle, Little Star' as I have never heard it before. A revelation. So beautiful! And it was followed by Mendelssohn's Concerto in E Minor. Amazing. A perfect end to the entertainment.

Dear old Richard's face was a picture. So pleased with himself. The 'Twinkle, Twinkle' thing had been all his own idea. Brilliant!

In the bar tonight Cameron told me that one of the best known exponents of Adam Baxter's 'Art' was someone from our own age called 'Jack the Rapper', who jumps out at people from dark corners in Whitechapel and assaults them with the following words.

The one called Jack the Ripper used a big sharp knife,
To creep up on the passers-by and cut away their life,
But I have found a better way of terminating breath,
It's far less messy rapping, I annoy them all to death.

Told him that Adam had offered to do another Rap in the Communion service tomorrow. Cameron clicked his fingers and tutted and said, 'Oh, no, what a shame! That's a real nuisance, Granddad. Thing is, I've been given this fantastic opportunity to be impaled on a metal spike and die in agony at the exact same time when the Communion's on, so obviously I wouldn't want to miss out on a once-only chance like that, would I? Still, you can't do everything, can you? Catch the Rap some other time, eh?'

Also had a chat with Gerald over a pint about my encounters with Community members, and their views of Alan Varney.

'Bit of a contrast in views between the different ones I met.'

Gerald said, 'Yes, I've spoken to several of them. I think I know more or less what's going on. This Varney character's a bit like my first vicar, you know, when I was a curate. David Corbett. Remember him? He had a little group around him who thought he was the best thing since Martin Luther. And as long as they did things the Corbett way he gave them good reason to love him. But anyone who disagreed or stood in the way of what he wanted to do was likely to be nailed to the church door. Bit of an exaggeration, but they did get very short shrift indeed.'

He held his finger and thumb up, about three millimetres apart.

'My shrift was about this long while I was there. I nearly got out of the Church altogether, if you remember. And the trouble with control freaks like Varney is that, in the end, all the people with ideas of their own are going to escape, drift away and leave him to be king of the castle. So he'll get more and more embedded into believing he's right, because there's no one left to argue with him. A gallon of power in a pint pot. That's what it boils down to, and I don't like it very much.'

He sighed.

'Shame he's the most important person in the world, isn't it? Blinking God! No taste in people.'

Text message from Leonard just before we went to bed tonight, as far as I can tell answering my earlier question about Scotch Corner. Do wish he wouldn't try to use abbreviated text, or whatever they call it. Takes forever to work out what he's talking about. This was his message: 'sry gt ct of. gt 2 sctch cnr cos hv md bd mstk. dint no thr wa 3 plasis cld stanwick n uk. hv bn 2 2 v thm. 1 lft mst b th rt 1 a? c u. hp u r ok. lv lnd n angls xx ps angls hs md it up wth kty.'

Aaaah, she's made it up with Katy. Sweet. Mad and totally meaningless, of course, but sweet.

When we got up to our room tonight Anne flopped back on the bed looking completely exhausted.

She hung a limp arm over the side of the bed and said, 'Adrian, I can't take another session with Sarah and Megan. It's harder work with them than without them. First thing in the morning, please will you smile at them, thank them, give them some money, and ask Richard or someone if they'd be kind enough to run them into the centre of Stanwick. That's where they live. It's not far. Couple of miles. Betty's offered to give me a hand tomorrow so I'll be fine. Will you do that for me?'

'Of course I will. Anne?'

Faint whisper.

'Yes?'

'I do enjoy being your husband.'

'Good. I enjoy being your wife.'

'Anne?'

'Yes, what is it?'

'You're lying across the bed. I can't get in.'

8

Sunday Morning

Tossed and turned all through the night, my head stuffed with trouble. Have an idea my brain was feverishly taking on any battle that might prevent me from allowing Josey to get to the front of the queue. First in line during most of the night was the prospect of tomorrow's final session.

I really cannot handle the idea of washing other people's horrible feet at this abominable plenary thing. To my mind all feet except a baby's are an abomination, especially when they're hard and horny and shaped all wrong. Suppose people had got athlete's foot or verrucas or bunions or ingrown toenails or they hadn't washed properly for a week? Ugh! Trouble is, in the middle of the night, even small things get bigger and bigger and worse and worse in your mind. During one period of fitful sleep I had a horrible dream in which a vast, misshapen, chiropodist's nightmare of a foot, about the size of Somerset, descended from the clouds like something out of Monty Python, and a voice boomed, 'Wash this diseased foot of mine or you can have no part of me.'

The same dream popped up three or four times throughout the early hours. After the final one I was about to start work on a bunion as big as the Quantocks with a tiny flannel and one of those aspirin-sized bars of soap you get in cheap hotels, when I woke in a cold sweat to find Anne about to put a mug of tea down next to me.

She said, 'Darling, what on earth were you dreaming about? You were moaning really loudly.'

'Moaning? I never moan in my sleep. What was I moaning about?'

'You were saying something like, "All right! All right! I'll wash it! Just tell me there isn't going to be another one!" I think that was it.'

'Oh, I think it's just this blessed plenary thing. You know how much I hate feet, but Thomas says the Holy Spirit really uses them, so I suppose . . .'

Anne threw her head back and laughed so long and loud that she spilt quite a lot of tea on my corner of the sheet. She recovered eventually.

She said, 'Oh, sweetheart, I'm so sorry. You didn't believe that nonsense of Gerald's, did you? How could you be alive and bumbling around the church all these years and still not know? I assumed you'd have sorted it out by now. A plenary session is just a time for everyone to get together at the same time and share what's been happening during the weekend – that sort of thing. Nothing to worry about. Not so much as a big toe in sight, I promise.'

Shuddered to the depths of my soul. How could a truly creative God be responsible for primroses, the aurora borealis *and* big toes? I suppose some mysteries will never be solved, not this side of the grave.

Bumbling around the church?

Anne kissed me very gently before going off to have a shower. I nearly gave in.

Came downstairs a bit later to find Sally the volunteer asleep in the dining-room. She had her head in a cardboard box on one dining-room chair, her feet in a second box on another chair and the rest of her under a blanket on two other chairs in between. Made her a cup of tea in the kitchen and woke her by tapping her softly on the shoulder. She sat up with the box still on her head, screamed and then slapped herself on the chest.

She said, 'Oh, sorry, I thought I'd been buried alive. It happened three times in the night. Waking up, I mean, not being buried alive. I have to keep my head and feet warm during the night, you see, and I couldn't think of any other way to do it. The warden had his family to stay unexpectedly, so I was going to have to move to twelve, but then they remembered it's got no ceiling at the moment, so they sent me off to forty, but forty was getting all the nasties from the toilet block next door. So I went all the way up to nine, then remembered that it can't be used until they drag out something or other that died in there last week. And sixteen, the last one they sent me to, seemed perfect until I found out my lights went out every time they flushed the loo in sixty-three. So I came down here. I don't mind all that much, but . . .'

Beautiful cooked breakfast this morning, served to me by my frying bustard friend with a brilliant smile and an extra egg. Strikes me that the bacon and egg combination must be one thing that somehow managed to avoid the corrupting effect of the fall. The benign creator must have looked at this divine combination of his when he first put it together, and seen that it was good. Very good. And he was right.

*   *   *

Sorted Megan and Sarah out after breakfast. They remained pallidly impassive, but I thought I detected a slight flicker as they registered the prospect of leaving early. Waved them off in the back of Richard's car, faces peering expressionlessly through the windows like Halloween masks drained of colour. Weird. Confusing. Demoralising. Glad they've gone.

I just can't understand Alan Varney. He came walking through the Moon Lounge where people were milling around or chatting after breakfast, and stopped when he saw a couple of the green-badged Community girls talking in a corner with their heads close together.

'If you're not mingling with guests you might as well go back to bed!'

An embarrassed hush fell over the room as the two girls shot to their feet and glanced around, red-faced, presumably trying to work out how to move from not mingling to mingling without the whole thing looking hollow and awkward. Fortunately, the little Swansea group includes two wonderful elderly ladies called Glenys and Mary, who are filled with physical pain and unquenchable goodwill. They had just started work again on a jigsaw puzzle over by the window. Glenys beckoned the girls over.

'You can mingle with Mary and me,' she called out. 'Don't you worry about him; I knew his grandfather, and he was a bad-tempered old devil as well. You come and help us with all this blue sky.'

Clever people have been poring over Scripture for two thousand years, trying to work out how to become like Glenys and Mary, regardless of how many Gods they believe in.

The atmosphere became comfortable once more. But why does he do it?

Quite a buzz before Father John's question time this morning. He looked so tired and frail sitting at the front in a big basket chair dragged in from the conservatory. Eyes still twinkling, though, just as they always did. Anne leaned across and whispered: 'When the smile's the only thing left he'll just float away to heaven, don't you think? I do love that old man.'

Bernard Masters, holding his big floppy Bible on his lap with lots of bits of paper sticking out of the sides, and two or three fingers keeping pages open as well, leaned his bony body forward and raised a hand.

'I would like to ask you, Father John, for your opinion on the homosexual question.'

Father John blinked in apparent bewilderment.

'I'm sorry – what exactly *is* the homosexual question?'

Masters jerked back and made a noise in his throat a bit like a printer getting paper scrunched up in its rollers.

'Errrrr, I mean, how do you view gay Christians?'

'Ah! I see. Yes, I think I understand now. How do I view gay Christians? Well, Bernard, I have to say that my stance on this matter has been formed and indeed dictated entirely by Scripture. And I should add that, although it is probably very wrong of me, I'm afraid I have very little patience with those who approach the issue in any other way. It makes me very cross. Again and again the Bible is quite unequivocal in its teaching on this issue.'

By now Masters had his fingers in so many pages of his Bible that he looked as if he was attempting to play some kind of strange, limp accordion.

'Well,' he said, 'my Bible makes it perfectly clear that . . .'

'Oh, yes indeed,' continued Father John as though Bernard hadn't spoken, 'I am absolutely committed to the biblical imperative you were about to mention.'

'Which is . . .?'

'Oh, just to love them, Bernard.'

The printer started to jam up again.

'Errrrr . . .'

'I suspect, you know,' went on the monk before the unblocking process could begin, 'that God is generally more shocked by our religion than by our sin. I am told that members of this lovely Community here at Scarleeswanvale Hall are obliged to promise, among other things, that they will do their best to treat guests as they would treat Jesus himself. I assume this is not intended to suggest that they should crucify them. I would counsel you all to avoid love-less disapproval like the plague. Because it is a plague like all the seven Egyptian ones lumped together. So is condem-nation. So is greed. There are far more heartlessly greedy folk in the Church than there are gay Christians. Read the Gospels in that amazing bespoke Bible of yours, Bernard. Ask yourself how we have allowed the preventable death of millions of children, and the descent into prostitution of little girls who perish before their ages reach double figures to become so much less of a sin than differences in sexuality.'

Silence for a moment or two, then Bernard recovered slightly.

'Are – are you saying that it's all right, then?'

Shrinking back into his chair, Father John seemed more frail and weary than ever as he replied.

'Oooh, scissors! Is *that* the homosexual question? Am I saying that it's all right? Is it all right? Is it all wrong? I wonder if it really matters what I am saying, Bernard? I am nothing but a tired, battered old Jesus-loving relativist, whatever that means. This beautiful, slightly irritating Saviour of ours moves from person to person doing this and that and the other and I, like the disciples of old, struggle to keep up and to do what I see him doing. He can be *so* inconsistent. Sometimes, when I quite fiercely quote Scripture at him he laughs at me. Once or twice I have shouted at him, "For goodness sake, why don't you get a *grip*!" This Master of mine has never been as easy to pin down as most of us would wish, and for that, I have to be honest, I thank God from the bottom of my heart.'

Happened to glance across at Gerald. Gave me a watery smile. I do love my son.

'Incidentally, Bernard,' said the monk, 'there is one other way in which I view gay Christians.'

'Ye-e-s?' croaked Bernard.

Father John's voice as he answered was very soft and layered with sadness.

'In the mirror.'

You could have heard the smallest pin drop on the softest pile of feathers.

'Many years ago I made a vow of celibacy when I joined the little order I belong to. It's very little. There aren't very many of us left. When you actually open your ears to God he usually speaks in a surprisingly gentle whisper. Elijah discovered that, didn't he? This was a very quiet, polite call to me, and I decided, mmm, I had better go. So – pain and frustration and joy and many other things. But the truth is . . .'

He chuckled quietly, and took a sip of water after coughing a little.

'I am an extravagant celibate, and I would rather praise God from the belly of a purpose-driven whale if that's where God has put me, than try unsuccessfully to stay asleep in the bottom of a storm-tossed ship that's going nowhere other than straight down to the place where strange, blind creatures crawl around in the dark. Those of us whose names begin with "J" have more than once reached that conclusion. Do you get my drift, Bernard?'

I think we all did . . .

Dear Betty Osbourne raised a hand nervously at one point. Father John raised both paper-thin hands to welcome her question.

'I'm sure this is a very silly question,' she said, 'but I've just been thinking about that bit in Ephesians where Paul talks about putting on the armour of God. You know, the helmet of salvation and the shield of whatsit and all the rest of them.'

Father John nodded encouragingly.

'It's just that I got a letter from my daughter Poppy last week. She's twenty-four and she works for one of these big Christian organisations, based right up in the north of England. She's had a bit of a difficult time lately, feeling very tired and not getting very much time off. Got really low, if you know what I mean. And that's not my lovely Poppy. She's bright and smiley usually, and she wants to be obedient to God. She really does. Always tries hard. Anyway, she kept it to herself for a few weeks, but one day she just

reached the end of her – whatever it is you reach the end of
– tether, is it? Thank you, yes, she reached the end of her
tether. And she told someone, one of the leaders I think it
was. And this lady, team leader or something, stood up very
stiff and straight and said to her, "You get up those stairs
my girl, and put on the armour of God!"'

Betty unfolded a sheet of paper and held it up.

'I'll read you what Poppy said in her letter. Really upset
me. Don't worry, it's not very long.

'"I went off upstairs like she told me, Mum, and I did
try to look at the piece about the armour, but I just ended
up crying instead and wishing you were there, so you
could put your arm round me and make me a cup of tea.
The armour didn't seem to work that afternoon, and I
wondered if I'd done something very wrong and God
was cross."'

Betty laid the letter down on her lap and looked hopefully at Father John.

'What do you think, Father John? What can I say to her?'

The benign smile had disappeared from Father John's
face. In fact, I've rarely seen him look so severe.

'Betty,' he said, his expression softening, 'I suspect that
dear Poppy's problem is a common one. There comes a
time for all of us when, whatever anyone else tells us to do,
and wherever they send us to do it, we become weary of
incessantly studying the recipe, and yearn for a little taste
of the food. That great man Dietrich Bonhoeffer spoke
about the possibility of achieving "religionless Christianity",
a state or place where we shall no longer require the assistance of maps or signposts because we have arrived, and the
place we have arrived at is our true home.

'Here's what I think, Betty. On that difficult, painful day, your Poppy didn't need to put on the armour of God. She needed to take it off. She had been wearing it bravely for a long time, and it was beginning to pinch and scrape, and weigh heavily on her. She needed a reminder of what the whole thing is about. A reminder of what the armour is for. Forgive my absurd cocktail of metaphors, but she deserved a little treat. A reminder of how good the real food tastes. A little taste of home to be going on with. And you know, in the end, a smile and a hug might have been enough. I am never judgemental,' (his eyes suddenly twinkled again), 'not like some other folks that I could name, but the people of God can be quite extraordinarily silly sometimes.

'As for God being cross with her – well, I don't *think* so, do you? I've seen poppies. They're so beautiful and fragile and open-faced and undervalued. Cross with Poppy? No, I don't think so.'

'Thank you,' said Betty, a little smile on her face as she folded her letter carefully and slipped it back into its envelope.

'Having said all that,' continued Father John, 'I do find Paul's words about the armour of God very helpful and useful. The belt of truth, for instance. The message is very clear. If you don't tell the truth you will end up embarrassed. Or, to put it another way, without a belt, your trousers will fall down. If Paul had been around in our age, I wonder if he would have encouraged us to also put on the braces of truth, just to make doubly sure.'

'What about us ladies?' asked Mrs Duphrane, cocking one eyebrow. 'We're not much into belts or braces.'

'Mmm, good question, my dear,' replied Father John, blinking thoughtfully, 'and I would certainly not wish you to suffer the unexpected descent of anything essential. I am more than a little out of date, however, and I have no personal or practical experience whatsoever of ladies' underwear, but I suppose it might have to be something like "the corsets of consistency", or possibly "the suspender-belt of spiritual sustenance".'

'Out of date?' whispered Anne with a smile, 'I should think he is. Hardly anyone wears braces nowadays, and I don't suppose there's a woman alive who wears either of those other items.'

'No,' I said absently, 'shame about the suspenders . . .'

Anne smacked my leg, then raised a hand.

'Father John, may I ask you a question?'

'Of course, Anne.'

'I've often wondered what Paul means . . .'

He interrupted with mock weariness.

'Oh, so have I, so have I!'

Little ripple of amusement. Bernard Masters glanced around in bewilderment.

'I've often wondered what he means in 2 Corinthians when he talks about a Christian he used to know who was taken up to the third heaven. Any idea what was going on there?'

'I may know the precise answer to that question before much longer,' replied Father John cheerfully, 'but in the meantime I'm really not sure. It does rather sound, doesn't it, as though this man was shot up in a lift, or "vertical personnel distributor", as I believe some of our American cousins call it. But what went on up in the room on that third floor is a mystery. We can guess, of course. Picture this mate of Paul's, sitting with Jesus on a balcony looking out over the world, as they share a chocolate fondue? Our Lord reminiscing about his trip to the lower ground floor to collect some of the folk who pressed the wrong button and ended up crying in the basement? Sounds perfectly feasible to me.'

'Will there be chocolate fondue in heaven?' asked Richard incredulously.

'Oh, Richard,' said Father John solemnly, 'do you seriously think I would have spent a lifetime turning my back on all sorts of delicious sins if I hadn't felt absolutely sure there was going to be chocolate at the end of it all? The shadowy figures of error and uncertainty may stalk most of us until our dying day, but there is no room for doubt when it comes to chocolate.'

Funny thing about Father John's way of talking. Don't quite know how to put it. The sense of what he says is not so much in the words as in something much deeper and stronger and more reassuring. It doesn't matter a bit whether there will actually be chocolate in heaven, because the essence of everything that's truly good is waiting up there on the third floor, chocolate as much as anything else.

Josey had a Bible open on her lap.

'Father John, it says here that the man heard "inexpressible things, things that man is not permitted to tell". That's so tantalising! I'm sure if I had something really interesting and important to tell everyone I'd want to splurge it out straightaway.'

Father John looked at her for a moment.

'Would you, my dear?'

Strange moment. Josey lowered her gaze, then looked up once more.

'I – I mean, I wonder what those inexpressible things could have been. It would be so exciting to know.'

'Ah,' said Father John, 'I would love to give you a bit of a hint about that. The trouble is that they are inexpressible. And to complicate things even more, they may well be different for each one of us.' He glanced at me. 'Adrian, for instance, would probably be happy to bat successfully against Michael Holding at Lord's for eternity. Others, particularly those who regard the watching of even one test match as an eternity of tedium might find that an excruciating prospect. God is very clever at all that sort of thing, though. He'll sort it out.'

Josey smiled, and then said, with a little catch in her voice, 'Will it all be all right?'

The most important question in the world. I drew a breath in and couldn't let it out until the answer came.

'Yes,' replied Father John – warmly, but almost in a whisper. 'Oh, *yes*.'

Just before we broke for coffee, Gerald asked a question.

'Earlier on, Father John, you said that there's too much greed in the Church. Does that mean it's wrong for Christians to be rich?'

'Yes and no, and no and yes,' replied the monk. 'Does that help?'

'Gosh yes,' Gerald nodded gravely '. . . and no. That pretty well clears it up altogether.'

'I suppose I mean my hope is that those who acquire lots of boodle won't bury it in a bank or a third house or something. I hope they'll be the sort of people who see themselves as bankers for God – forgive me for using the "b" word – good *stewards* for God. Nothing wrong with that. I'm glad they're the ones who've got it to give away. Lots of chances to give treats as well. I love treats, don't you – especially chocolate, wine, stories told to me by children?'

A sea of enthusiastic nods. He stirred in his chair, thinking something through for a moment.

'The other "no" and "yes" was about getting rich in a different sort of way, and speaking of treats, let me tell you about my pig. You see, I share my room at home with a great big pig. And before you ask, it's not one of the other brothers, they're a completely different variety of animal. No, it's an enormous, gorgeously ugly piggy bank. About two feet tall. Given to me as a birthday present a few years ago by a lovely family who live nearby and know how much I enjoy going out to tea. We don't have very much money of our own in the order, but I do love to collect coins in my pig. This is how I do it.

'Every time someone is especially kind to me I go upstairs at the end of the day and put a little bit of money in my pig. I try not to think about how much has gone in, so that I will be wildly surprised and excited when I eventually count it. I usually take the money out every few months and take it down to one of those supermarkets where there's a machine that turns your shrapnel into something more manageable. Rather satisfying. I use the money to give my brothers a special treat. We've been ten-pin bowling, which is great fun and an, um, interesting thing to do when you're wearing a habit like mine; we've gone out all together for a pizza – ham and pineapple for me; we've been to the local cinema to watch mildly inappropriate films; and all sorts of things. All those treats paid for with acts of kindness. I love it.

'And the thing is – I may be wrong, but I suspect each one of us has a sort of piggy bank in heaven. If you read the sixth chapter of Matthew's Gospel you'll see that every time we do something good and kind and right God puts a bit of money in for us. Jesus said, didn't he, that we should store up treasure in heaven. I don't know if Pizza Hut have a branch in paradise, but I do think we shall have a lot of fun spending our savings. So yes, spend love generously and extravagantly. Let your account grow. Ching ching! God's financial institutions are a lot safer than any old Icelandic bank, I can assure you.'

I had a final thing to ask. I didn't expect an answer.

'Father John, why does God allow horrible things to happen to people who trust and believe in him?'

This impossible question seemed to have dropped into a dark abyss as the elderly monk gazed out of the window, his face more grey and etched with pain than ever. At last he spoke, very gently and carefully.

'Because – because he is too loving and too unselfish to do otherwise.'

There was no more time, but those words rang out like a distant, oddly familiar bell as we rose to our feet and began making our way towards the chapel.

There were four noteworthy items in our otherwise fairly conventional Communion service. One was the drama organised by Thomas Grimaldi with a group of children. This was noteworthy because it should never have happened.

I do really wish people would listen to me when I say

things. I distinctly remember telling George Farmer, when he offered to organise a drama for the service, that it would be a bad idea to take up ancient Mr Grimaldi on his offer to get involved. Then I forgot about it, and of course George wasn't at the planning meeting . . . Thomas Grimaldi joined us from a church west of ours called St Yorick's, in order to be 'closer to Italy'. It works out at three miles closer. His previous vicar warned Dennis that Mr Grimaldi is obsessed with the role and history of Italy in the Second World War, and particularly by the execution of Benito Mussolini. Just before the service began I learned that, for some insane reason, George agreed that he could prepare a separate little drama in the service with some of the young children and teach them a song. Why do some people give in to other people so easily?

Shrank down in my chair on the front row, dreading the moment when Grimaldi and his small troupe were due to appear.

When it came to the 'little drama' it was like something out of one of those ghastly Tarantino films that Gerald used to enjoy so much. Horrified to see a gang of four or five children dragging a life-sized dummy made of clothes stuffed with newspaper to the centre of the service space, putting a noose round its neck and suspending it from a primitive gallows lugged on and erected by Grimaldi and a small, stern girl with pigtails. The whole group cheered and waved their fists and sang the following words two or three times with enormous gusto.

We drag the filthy fascist from his bed, bed, bed,
Then we hang him from a lamp-post 'til he's dead,
    dead, dead!

Widespread shock and consternation at this hideous spectacle from parents and others who had perhaps been expecting something more along the lines of 'The wheels on the bus go round and round'. Wondered how Grimaldi was going to fit this abomination into the theme of the service. He grabbed a microphone from a stand and addressed the congregation like some sort of guerrilla leader mustering troops for an attack on Rome.

'Anda so we see alla the weeked ones musta face justeece ina the enda. Mussolini anda Satan heemaself willa bow to the powerr of love thata conquerrs alla! *La vittoria al potere di amore!* Amen!'

I think this sentence in Italian means something like 'Victory to the power of love.' Oddly and unexpectedly impressive in the end, though I suspect Grimaldi was more interested in the power than the love. I could only imagine what one or two of the parents might have to say about their kids miming a public execution. I remember someone saying that, generally speaking, Christians are only happy to be spiritually fed if their food has been sliced, diced and preferably even chewed before it gets to them. Grimaldi's offering was quite a long way towards the other end of the spectrum. More like a big, hard block of stale old bread that had to be bolted and digested in one.

The second noteworthy thing was Father John's sermon. Quite an air of expectancy as he made his way forward to preach. Sitting there at the front he looked like a discarded coat piled carelessly on a stool, but his eyes shone with the calm, uncomplicated wisdom of a much-loved child. This is what he said:

Thank you so much for asking me to say some words at your Communion service. I don't do much of this sort of thing anymore, but I've known one of your lovely churches for a good many years now, and I am confident that you will be kind enough to search diligently through my rubbish in case there is anything worth looking at and recycling or thinking about for a little while.

This morning I would like us all to consider doing two things. First of all we might like to thank God very much indeed for the way in which he – how can I put it? – he continually cuts us some slack. I think that's the expression I'm looking for.

Let me tell you one of the great stories from the Old Testament. This is a tale that most of you will already know really well. It's the story of an army commander. He was called Naaman. I do tend to take a few liberties with biblical text, so if you want to follow this passage and keep a close track of my heresies, Bernard, you'll find it in the fifth chapter of the second book of Kings.

Flicker and flurry of turning pages from Bernard's direction, and little murmurs of recognition from many of the listeners, including me. I remember making this Naaman character out of a bit of cornflake packet at Sunday School sixty years ago, and dipping him into a sink filled with water when I got home to see if the leprosy spots I'd painted onto his body would be washed off. They sort of were, but I wouldn't have called him clean exactly, more soggy and stained.

Father John continued,

I think Naaman was probably a good man. After all, he listened to the advice of children and servants. That's always a good sign. And his master, the king of a country called Aram, seemed to value him very highly. Wrote a useful letter for him to take to Israel, and loaded him with all sorts of treasure to offer Elisha the prophet in return for sorting out a horrible disease that must have been a bit like what we call leprosy.

Perhaps Naaman was just a *little* bit too big for his boots. When Elisha didn't even bother coming out to meet him, and sent a mere servant with a message telling him to bathe seven times in the River Jordan, he turned his nose up and got cross.

'I'm not bathing in your nasty, smelly old river,' he said. 'We've got a couple of great big wonderful clean ones of our own back home that make your rotten, stinky Jordan look like a poisonous little trickle. Anyway, this so-called prophet of yours didn't even have the good manners to come out and talk to me when I arrived. I'm a very important man, you know. I could cause a lot of trouble for people around here if I wanted to, and I might just want to! Well, blow him and his bathing-seven-times-in-a-muddy-puddle nonsense! I'm off home!'

And away he went, stroppy as anything, back towards Aram, still a leper. Like I said, though, there must have been some real good in this man, because his servants weren't afraid to tell him what they thought.

'Now look, master, you didn't go there to get a pat on the back,' they said. 'You went there to get healed. And you want to be healed. We want you to be healed. Why don't you turn round, find a nice flat bit of bank down by the river, hold your nose if it makes you feel better, and do what the prophet said?'

So he went. Seven times he dipped himself down among the presumably rather puzzled fish, and after the seventh time he *was* healed. And he was *very, very* happy, and enormously grateful. 'I'm going to worship the God of Israel from now on,' he declared when he went back to thank Elisha, who must have come out to see him this time. 'You say you won't take any gifts, which is a shame, but if it's OK I am going to take a load of earth from your country, and use it to kneel down on whenever I want to praise this amazing God of yours who has given me back the clean flesh of a young boy.'

So, that was all fine and dandy, wasn't it? But it's the next bit I want us to get our heads round this morning. You see, Naaman was just about to set off happily again towards Aram when he stopped, looked a bit troubled, scratched his chin, and spoke to Elisha once more.

'Er, a bit of a problem.' He said.

'Spit it out, then,' replied Elisha – that's how prophets talked in those days, you understand.

Bernard Masters stirred uneasily, and almost wrote something in his notebook.

'The thing is,' went on Naaman, 'when I get back home my master the king will be expecting me to go into the temple of Rimmon with him (Rimmon is our local god, whom I don't believe in any more, in case you haven't heard of him), and when the king bows down, you see, I'll have to bow down as well, because he'll be leaning on my arm as usual. So, my question is – well, is it OK to do that? Or not. Or what? Have I got to make a stand?'

Father John paused and looked around the meeting room.

'So, was it OK – or not? Or what? What do you think?'

Another silence.

'I have a sort of feeling,' he continued whimsically, 'that quite a lot of Christians in this gloriously enlightened age of ours might say, when faced with the same question about a similar situation, "Oh no! Not a chance. Servants of the one true God do *not* compromise. They stand up for what they believe, whatever the consequences." Which makes it all the more interesting and slightly surprising that Elisha answered Naaman's question with these three words: "Go in peace."

'That was all he said, and it seemed to be all that was needed on that particular occasion. Through a prophet who was more interested in hearing the authentic whisper of the Holy Spirit than blindly following patterns and preconceptions, God was cutting Naaman a little slack, and this new follower of the one true God was probably even more grateful than before, don't you think? How lovely to be told you can go in peace when you are expecting a thick ear or a thunderbolt.'

Father John looked around the room again. Anne said later that he seemed to be struggling to organise an unruly passion within himself. His eyes shone with unshed tears as he spoke.

'My dear, dear friends, I cannot think of three more beautiful words in the whole of the universe. And only one person has the authority to actually make them mean what they say, and give what they offer. When I go into my room in the evening to tell Jesus that I have messed up yet again, he smiles at me with such affection, and he says, "John, my friend, your sins are forgiven. Go in peace." And then a miracle happens. I am totally without sin for, oh, it can be as long as half a second sometimes. But the smile – oh, the smile lasts for much, much longer. Where is the love? It's there – in that smile.

'Please let God cut you some slack. Set out to do your very best today, and when the night comes and you have failed to hit the mark, just say to him, "I'm really sorry, I've tried, but I can't quite get there at the moment." And he will reply, "It's OK. Relax. We'll talk tomorrow. Sleep well. *Go in peace.*"'

The very air seemed to groan with an unspoken question.

Can that really, honestly be true?

Father John's eyes swept the room again.

'Some of us find that *so* hard to believe, don't we? Well, those of us who can't survive on a guilt-free diet don't need to worry. If the thick ear or the thunderbolt is what we really want or need to feed on, he's quite capable of cooking that up.'

Quite an outburst of relieved laughter. Anne leaned across and whispered, 'Why does the prospect of being freed from guilt worry us all so much?'

'The other thing I'd love us to do is to cut God some slack. He does work awfully hard on our behalf, you know, mostly behind the scenes, and much of the time the results don't look very impressive. We pray for sick people and they die. We ask God to intervene and he doesn't. We yearn for deep peace and find ourselves either filled with or surrounded by a raging storm. We long to have someone special to love and it just doesn't happen. We cry out to know why he has forsaken us, and there is no answer. Despite having all those angels at his disposal, he leaves us on the cross. Not being able to give us what we want breaks his heart sometimes, not least because he took such a wounding in order to give us what we need. Do try not to make his pain worse. Cut him a little slack, eh? I think it will be OK in the end. As I come near to the last days of my life I feel more sure than ever that, as jolly old Julian wrote, possibly while lingering over an Americano in the St Andrew's Crypt coffee shop in beautiful Norwich, all manner of things will definitely be well.

'"Go in peace to love and serve the Lord." That's what the priest says as the Communion service comes to an end. And they are wise words. Without the balm of forgiveness and the promise of peace we shall not endure the pain of love and service. I can testify to that. Amen.'

As Father John climbed creakily from his stool, Duncan Whitton at the piano plunged, without any introduction, into the opening bars of that wonderful hymn 'It is Well with my Soul' written by Horatio Spafford in 1873 as he sailed over the part of the Atlantic where his four daughters had drowned on their way from America to Europe. Anne and I glanced at each other. Spafford's brave, wild, foolishly wise words have always broken our hearts. They did now, especially after listening to Father John. Hearts in tatters all around the room. And Duncan played with such passion.

You would never have expected it from a man so mild.
Perhaps, for him, it was a fresh expression. (Maybe I should
ask Alvin Dekkle what he thinks.) The words of the hymn
came up on a screen, but I almost know them by heart.

When peace, like a river, attendeth my way,
When sorrows like sea billows roll;
Whatever my lot, Thou has taught me to say,
It is well, it is well, with my soul.

It is well, with my soul,
It is well, with my soul,
It is well, it is well, with my soul.

Though Satan should buffet, though trials should come,
Let this blest assurance control,
That Christ has regarded my helpless estate,
And hath shed His own blood for my soul.

It is well, with my soul,
It is well, with my soul,
It is well, it is well, with my soul.

My sin, oh, the bliss of this glorious thought!
My sin, not in part but the whole,
Is nailed to the cross, and I bear it no more,
Praise the Lord, praise the Lord, O my soul!

It is well, with my soul,
It is well, with my soul,
It is well, it is well, with my soul.

And Lord, haste the day when my faith shall be sight,
The clouds be rolled back as a scroll;
The trump shall resound, and the Lord shall descend,
Even so, it is well with my soul.

It is well, with my soul,
It is well, with my soul,
It is well, it is well, with my soul.

By the time that swelling chorus filled the room a second time I could hardly stop the tears from coming. Feeling the slight weight of Josey leaning very gently against my shoulder, I prayed inside like a frightened child.

'God – Father, if that's what you really are. Make everything all right. Don't let Father John die and disappear and not exist any more. Please be there to smile and take his hand and show him the place you've got ready for him. And look after all my special people. Anne and Gerald and Cameron and Josey. Josey, Lord. I don't think it's going to be well with our souls if she dies. Don't let her die. And if she does – well, just don't let her. And Leonard and Angels and all our friends. Lots of them aren't very good at Christianity, Father. In fact they're rubbish at it really. We all are. Please look after us and, if it's possible, put a hymn in our hearts when the bad times come. Help us to be honest and brave like Jesus. I don't want to be a useless "Christian" any more. I want to be with him and you – and them. Forever.'

Not a very good prayer, and certainly not a very tidy one, but I did *so* mean it.

*   *   *

Noteworthy event number three was the Communion itself, led with great vigour and clarity by the Scarleeswanvale chaplain. For me, Communion always is noteworthy, but this one . . . I was first in line, so I was able to come back to my seat and watch all the others as they trooped up to the rail. There they were, queuing up for a taste of heaven, hoping for the best, but more or less ready to cling on to whatever they were given or could bring themselves to take. All those different heights and depths of passion and empti-ness and fear and belief and doubt and excitement and dull despair.

Gerald and Josey and Cameron and Anne and Richard and Minnie and Betty and Mrs Duphrane and Reg and Polly and her boys and Duncan and annoying Alvin and the rest of them, all reaching into the darkness and hoping against hope that the tips of their fingers might brush the very edge of his garment of light. It made me cry. It always does.

Then, a brilliant finish to the service. We did the Exchanging of the Peace right at the end, accompanied by a recording of the wonderful Marti Webb, putting every-thing into her glorious rendition of 'Blow, Gabriel, Blow!' More like a party than anything else.

Astonished, when I looked through the window just after the milling started, to see Leonard and Angels hurrying away towards the car park. Must have slipped in at the back just after the beginning of the service. Took me some time to get through the clumps of chattering, peace-exchanging people (including Richard Cook, who wanted to talk to me about the fact that Julian of Norwich couldn't possibly have been drinking an Americano because they didn't exist when 'he' was alive), and by the time I got to the parking area Leonard's car was disappearing in a cloud of exhaust fumes round the corner towards the main road. Why did they rush off like that after taking so long to get here?

Before we started the prayer ministry in the Hexagonal Lounge after coffee Anne said, 'Adrian, I've been thinking that you and I ought to make more space for the Holy Spirit when people come for prayer. And I'm getting a bit sick of offering God a summary of our conversation after we've listened to people, just in case he's missed any of the important points. How would it be if, just for once, we try not to say anything unless we've actually got something to say?'

Sounded a bit radical to me, but I went along with the idea. Sometimes think Anne and God have a bit of a thing going when it comes to making decisions. I tend not to get consulted in the planning stages. So much for Ephesians, eh?

First person to join us in our little triangle of chairs was Mrs Duphrane. Sat in her chair very straight-backed and still, looking out of the window across the fields and saying nothing. Suddenly realised I had no idea what her Christian name was. Names are written very small on the badges supplied by Scarleeswanvale. Makes it a bit awkward, especially when you're a man and you find yourself peering closely at one side of a lady's chest. I don't have the sheer cheek Gerald had when he was younger, asking women cheerfully, 'What's the other one called?' Anne used to get quite cross about this, but I don't remember anyone taking offence.

Problem when you're about to pray for someone and you don't know who they are, is that you have to keep finding substitutes for the name when you're praying for them.

'Lord, we bring before you our dear sister here . . .' (*whose name we don't know*)

'Father, your servant is in great need . . .' (*of a much larger name badge*)

'Lord, you know this child of yours so much better than we do . . .' (*you can say that again*)

'We know that her name is written in the book of life . . .' (*any chance of you texting it through?*)

Anne said, 'Mrs Duphrane, I'm so sorry, but I don't think I know your first name.'

A-a-a-a-ah, clever! Never thought of that . . .

Mrs Duphrane turned her head to look at Anne for a moment, and replied quietly and clearly, 'My name is Daphne.' She smiled faintly. 'Yes, it is a bit like finding a trilobite, isn't it? Sorry, interest of mine. Trilobite. Extinct marine arthropod of the class Trilobita, of the Paleozoic Era, found in fossil form throughout the world. We Daphnes will probably be extinct within a few years. All of us dry old fossils. Dried up and extinct.'

Turned her face and stared out of the window again.

Felt we really ought to say something. Glanced at Anne, but she just did a tiny shake of her head. Seemed like about three years before Daphne Duphrane turned to us again. Her face was expressionless, but a single large tear spilled out of one eye like a liquid boulder, trickled down her cheek and landed with a tiny 'splish!' on the back of one liver-spotted hand.

'I am alone, and lonely,' she said bleakly. 'Thomas was my friend and my husband, and we were not able to have children. Thomas was the first and very probably the last person to love me, to laugh with me, and to hold me when the darkness that is deeper than night creeps into my soul. I am awfully rich and well appointed, but nowadays I feel like one of those grand, poorly maintained Edwardian mansions that you see in oil-rich ex-Soviet republics. I am fading and cracking, subsiding like a wing of a house that sinks into the ground because all the moisture has been sucked from the clay beneath it. Forgive me. Disgusting metaphor.'

She paused. I glanced helplessly at Anne once more, but her face was expressionless.

'I know there is no God,' continued Daphne, 'and I am – lost.'

Anne said softly, 'Why did you come away for this weekend, Daphne?'

She dabbed at her eyes with a lace handkerchief taken from an expensive sleeve, one side of her mouth twitching and dropping a little as she replied.

'Your son. Gerald. He is a glimmer of light.'

My son is a glimmer of light? My son is a glimmer of light.

'So silly . . .' She chuckled hoarsely. 'And so – full of an unusual variety of friendly, conversational loving-ness. He is also a bad golfer, as I always was in the days – Thomas and I loved to play an occasional round, but I was never any good.'

Anne and I glanced at each other. She signalled 'Don't ask!' with one eyebrow.

'I happened to be in a big red tomb-like church down behind our ghastly Gents toilet of a bus-station to witness a despatching or a hatching or something. Might as well have been in Asda. Prefer Asda. More choice of aisles, more choice all round – and they don't expect you to sing. But your Gerald was the guest preacher. Must have been friendly with the stars of the show, I suppose.

'He spoke in his sermon about why he continues to be a Christian when things are dark and unpromising. It's like playing putrid golf, he said. (Pricked my ears up, as you can imagine – not what I was expecting.) Every now and then, in the middle of a miserably unsuccessful round, just as you know you've decided once and for all that you might as well throw your clubs into the nearest pond to share a watery grave with scores of your old golf balls, you suddenly do a near perfect chip onto the thirteenth green. And everything changes. The contact of iron on ball is so sweet, so perfect, so utterly and exactly a representative capsule of this sorry world as it was always meant to be, that you say to yourself, "Oh, how I *love* this wonderful, wonderful game! If I can play a shot like that once – just once, then there is at least a skinny chance that I might do it again. And again! And over and over again! I *love* golf!"

'"In the end," he said, "bearing all that in mind, following Jesus seems to be the best game in town, so I think I'll carry on with it for a while. Hope to make some reasonable shots. Dreaming of a hole in one, one of these days. Keep going until I get to the clubhouse."

'That's what he said. Later, when he was shaking my hand in the porch I said, "Where and when do you tee off usually?" Sharp. Read my mind perfectly. "Eleven o'clock at St Jim's," he said. "Don't come to the nine-thirty. Half of them dress like failed Jehovah's Witnesses and the other half worship as though they're about to be hung. Come to the eleven o'clock. Like a bus queue that's moved indoors. Much more interesting." So I started going. Still go. Don't believe in any of it. But I believe a bit in Gerald. He makes me laugh, is occasionally very slightly and satisfactorily coarse, and he is terribly serious about not taking himself too seriously. That's why I go. He is a – glimmer.'

The bleak curtain started to fall once more as she turned her face to the window. Felt a panic-stricken need to say something – anything – to make God happen for Daphne. No words came. Hadn't got any. I have trouble enough making him happen for me. Horrified when I suddenly started crying like a baby. Just couldn't stop. Then Anne started. Moments later Daphne turned and put her arms out towards us. Her bottom lip began to tremble and she burst into tears. In the end all three of us just held on to each other and wept for ages. Never known anything like it.

Never did get round to actually praying – did we?

Afterwards, when we were all a bit less damp, Daphne Duphrane said, 'Well, that was a little bizarre, to say the least, but I suspect it was rather good for all four of us.'

I said, 'Three of us, you mean.'

Both of them looked at me as if I was a small, quaint child.

My life seems to be largely occupied with two types of journey. One is the continual struggle to get back to square one. At its crudest this means, for instance, that if I offer to clear away after a meal I am quite likely to knock over a glass of red wine (it will always be red), and spend the next ten minutes – or more if I am immediately offered six wildly varying opinions on the best way to clean it up – working frantically away to reach the point where I can begin the thing I was actually aiming to do in the first place. The other type of journey is that oft-frequented little bit of road that leads directly from the sublime to the ridiculous, and that was how it felt moving from our encounter with Daphne to the only other person Anne and I prayed for this morning.

It was a man from Gerald's church who introduced himself on Friday evening as 'Downton Grange – not a house, a person.'

Downton is a stocky, good-natured chap with a blond crew-cut and a strong Black Country accent. Told us he's lived most of his life in Tipton, 'where the zoo is'. No trouble opening up this time. 'My problem,' he said, 'is that every now and then I find myself speaking and behaving exactly like Neil Kinnock. Remember? The bloke with the red hair who fell down on the beach and it was all over the telly and it didn't do him much good.'

No need this time to restrain ourselves from trotting out platitudes. On the contrary, a good solid platitude would have come in handy. Nodded solemnly for a minute or so. Tried to look as if helpful, Spirit-inspired thoughts were gradually percolating through. The ridiculous question I came out with in the end was so crass and irrelevant that I blush to remember it.

'So, Downton,' I enquired gravely, 'are you yourself a member of the Labour Party?'

He seemed to take the question very seriously.

'That's what's so odd,' he said. 'I've got no socialist lean-ings and no connections at all with Wales, other than a deep and burning ambition concerning Snowdon.'

Completely out of my depth.

Anne said, 'Downton, it's nearly lunchtime. I think we'll just say a prayer for you now and pray again later, perhaps?'

Anne prayed that Downton would be released from any compulsion to take on Kinnock-like attributes. Managed to contain a sort of mad laugh that rose from my belly as she said the words. As we all intoned 'Amen' the five-minute lunch bell sounded. As we walked towards the dining room Downton said, 'Do you know, I think I'm healed. No, I'm *sure* I'm healed. Thank you both so much.'

Rather chuffed by this, ludicrous though it seemed at the time. Said casually to Gerald before lunch, 'By the way, bit of a result with one of your fellows just now. Chap called Downton Grange . . .'

'Not a house, a person?'

'Yes, that's right. He reckons he was healed of some obsession with Neil Kinnock when Mum and I prayed for him.'

'Oh, good. He was healed when I prayed for him as well. That's the second time with me I think. And a couple of times last month when someone else had a go. Happens all the time, I'm afraid. Scratch a problem, find a lost child. I'm going down to Wales with him next year to walk up Snowdon.'

'Is that what he really wants, then?'

He considered for a moment.

'No. But it'll do for now.'

Funny when you discover there are things about your own son that you never knew at all.

9

Sunday Afternoon

Very good Sunday lunch. Said to Gerald as we came out of the dining-room, 'I was just thinking about you taking on that young bloke who was so rude to Gladys on Friday. Aren't you worried you'll get yourself hung one of these days?'

He said, 'As long as I've really earned it I don't mind. Anyway, with Josey's style of unedited feedback I can't go too far wrong. She's a tough guy. Never pulls punches.'

Felt my mouth moving without any words coming out. Had to think of something to actually say.

'Oh, one thing I meant to tell you was that Daphne Duphrane says you're a glimmer.'

'Oh. Not a flashlight, then?'

'No, a glimmer.'

'Not a fairly powerful torch?'

'No, no, a glimmer.'

'Not a tiny, but occasionally useful torch with a very narrow beam like the ones you sometimes have on your key ring?'

'No, just a glimmer.'

He smiled.

'OK, I'll settle for that. Thanks, Dad.'

Explained a little more about what had happened and asked Gerald if he thought it mattered that Anne and I hadn't actually prayed with Daphne Duphrane.

He said, 'You know how everyone quotes John 3:16 all over the place?'

'Yes, what about it?'

'I've found another 3:16. It's in Malachi.'

'What does it say?'

'Well, you know how Malachi is one long rant by the creator about being offered second-rate stuff all the time. I suppose nowadays we'd say "God doesn't appreciate garage flowers." Something like that.'

Thought about it for a moment.

'Right.'

'OK, so in the end some people got together and talked about how they could put things right. And Malachi 3:16 says that God received their conversation as prayer. Neat, eh?'

Another moment.

'Very neat. Very neat indeed.'

Text came through from Leonard and Angels shortly after that.

Sorry had 2 rush off. There just in time hear Father J's talk. Must have bin a grt weekend if all like that. Had hurry. Took 3 days get here so won't gt back home til late in week. Angels falln in luv with Katy's frnd the Irishman. Shes bind th AA map 2 stp him gtting jellus. Thnk its only a crush. See soon. L & A xxxx

Plenary session in the Hexagonal Lounge just after lunch. Lots of people keen to get away and begin their homeward journeys, but I promised it wouldn't take more than half an hour and they all turned up.

Dennis surfed elegantly in with a prayer at the beginning,

and then I threw the meeting open to anyone who wanted to comment on the weekend. I said that, even though Anne and I had organised the weekend, we were both keen to hear negative responses as well as positive ones so that we could do better in future. Anne nodded when I made this statement, and I know she meant it. As far as I was concerned, it was a complete lie. I hate all criticism, especially the constructive sort, because then you have to do something about it. Just had to hope for the best.

Nothing too bad in the end. An elderly man from Gerald's church complained that because one of the legs of his bed was fractionally smaller than the other three, he had for two nights running dreamt that he was a ball bearing rolling along a flat wooden surface in one of those games in a box where you have to twist two knobs at the same time to stop the ball from dropping into a hole as you manoeuvre it along a winding path towards the finishing line.

Asked if this had put him off coming again.

He said, 'Yes, absolutely. Well, no. Actually, on reflection I rather enjoyed my dreams and I would like to be allocated the same bed on the next occasion. I withdraw my complaint.'

There were one or two comments about the way the children's work began on Friday, but far more compliments and an actual round of applause for the great job Anne had done since Friday evening, and Betty's contribution this morning. My Anne, eh? Nobody mentioned Thomas Grimaldi's little drama. Not that he would have noticed it much if they had. I think that inside his head he is firmly resident in the fifth decade of the last century.

One interesting thing. Halfway through the session Enid Struthers cleared her throat nervously and raised a hand.

'Yes, Enid. Did you want to say something?'

'Yes, I do have something to say.'

She paused and then said, in a manner probably more dramatic than she had intended, 'I have been a vengeful woman.'

She bowed her head for a moment or two, then looked up, twisting her interlinked fingers together over and over again as she spoke.

'I have always – all my life I have exchanged hurt for hurt, insult for insult, neglect for neglect. It always seemed to me that I had the right, the absolute right to balance the scales, as it were. Why should people think that they could cheat me or do bad things to me and not expect to receive the same in return? It seemed to me a sort of universal law. I became . . .'

Once more she dropped her eyes for an instant.

'I became very good at it. From childhood onwards I have been proficient with words, and I have used that ability to attack others and to defend myself.'

She sighed deeply.

'I may be foolish, but I am not stupid. I understood exactly what Father John was really saying to me at that meeting after I was so spiteful about Eamonn and Patrick, whom I can see now are two normal, lovely boys with a hard-working mother who deserves to be supported and not criticised.'

She threw a tentative glance at Polly Cluskey.

'I am so *very* sorry, Polly. I hope – I was hoping that you might have noticed a change in – a difference since then between – well . . .'

Clearly, Enid's proficiency with words had temporarily deserted her, but she had no need to worry.

'Oh yes!' said Polly warmly. 'I was so glad to see you playing Scrabble with the boys earlier. They are naughty sometimes, but they've got good hearts. Actually, I was wondering why your attitude had changed so much since . . . oh, dear! – that's dreadfully rude. I'm so sorry!'

She clapped her hands against reddened cheeks, but Enid was joining in with the chorus of laughter that had greeted Polly's embarrassed effusion.

'No, you mustn't worry, dear. I don't blame you in the slightest. And thank you so much for saying that you have noticed a change. Father John was quite right. I had read those words in the Lord's Prayer thousands and thousands of times – read them, but never seen them. Now I have, and I am so glad, and – just a little excited.'

Lorna and William Ebson also offered a major contribution. They insisted on coming out to the front. Held hands as they spoke – at first. As far as I can remember – and I have double-checked with Gerald – this is what they said:

LORNA: William and I would like to say a few words if that's OK with everybody, wouldn't we, William?

WILLIAM: Yes, we . . .

L: Most of you will not be aware that our marriage has been under some strain recently. Naturally, we never advertise the tensions in our relationship (*a frisson of sheer wonder passed around the room*) but we have to confess that they do exist, and indeed we have had to deal with some issues during this weekend. Have we not, William?

W: Yes, and . . .

L: I would like to make it quite clear that the fault has been largely mine.

William was not invited to support or contradict this statement. He did open his mouth to say something, but wasn't quite quick enough to get it out.

L: I have failed to understand and absorb that wonderful passage of Scripture in the book of Ephesians where wives are commanded to submit to their husbands. Haven't I, William?

W: You certainly . . .

L: From this day onwards I intend to spend a great deal more time under my husband's mantle.

W: (*his eyes popping*) Really?

'*More* time?' whispered Gerald.

L: For his part, I am sure that William is intending to work hard towards becoming the head of his wife as Christ is head of the Church.

W: If I . . .

L: For my own . . .

W: (*pulling his hand away from Lorna's*) *If* I might be allowed to interrupt your humble submission for long enough to actually say a word or two, I would suggest that most of the work needs to be done by *you*, my darling, as I am already doing my very best to be like Christ in your life.

L: (*aghast pause*) I'm sorry. *You* are claiming to be like Christ in my life?

W: I think so, yes.

L: Oh! Well, let me just think about this. Yes, you certainly are like Christ in the sense that I never see you, you hardly ever speak to me, you tend to be somewhere else at times when you're most needed, you never share your plans or ideas with me, you hang around with a scruffy bunch of men who are obsessed with fishing and never do any work, and you enjoy the company of highly questionable women. Yes, you're like Christ all right.

w: (*after a short pause*) And you, *sweetheart*, are like the beloved one spoken of in Solomon's Song of Songs.

L: (*somewhat taken aback*) Oh! In what way?

w: Song of Songs, chapter one, verse nine: 'I liken you, my darling, to a mare.'

L: Well, if you think I'm going to stand here and . . .

w: You don't have to. Sit down for a bit and I'll carry on. Actually, no, you don't have to do that. Why don't you go and have a gallop round the paddock. I'll get your size eighteen nosebag ready for when you come back.

L: Right! That does it! If you think for one moment . . .

w: That's longer than you've ever managed in the past.

Fortunately, Dennis abandoned his elaborate triple-moated sandcastle to intervene at this point. Otherwise they might have ended up rolling around on the floor. Is this the end for the Ebsons or, as Gerald believes, just an unconscious, convoluted way of organising yet another passionate reconciliation? We shall see.

Things went downhill for a while just after that.

Downton Grange (not a house, a person) told everyone that he believed he had finally broken free from Neil Kinnock, an announcement that must have been profoundly, possibly disturbingly inexplicable to those in the group who had no idea what he was talking about. There was a bewildered round of applause and Minnie Stamp got up and went over to kneel beside Downton, tilting not only her head, but just about everything else that was tiltable, while she gave him one of her dying-flower smiles and stroked his arm in a vaguely pastoral sort of way. Downton patted her hand in return and thanked her quietly, but I noticed that he did so in a gravelly Welsh accent. Not a problem. I have a sort of feeling he'll be miraculously healed when Minnie prays for him after the plenary session. Mind you, if Minnie Stamp transfers her attention to him, he's really going to miss old Neil.

Daphne Duphrane cleared her throat just as we were coming to the end of the half hour. She spoke with her usual elegance, but there was a softness that we had not heard before.

'This weekend has taught me something about myself that I would not have believed possible.'

An interested hush fell. I don't suppose public vulnerability has ever been easy for Daphne, but it is a wonderful spectator sport for those who happen to be present when it happens.

'I have learned, rather to my own surprise, that the seeds of belonging have been planted in me. By whose hands? I have only the faintest notion. What manner of flowering should I anticipate? A deep but roseate mystery. I am quietly pleased. Yes, very quietly. But, yes, pleased.'

In this crystalline moment I noticed Alvin Dekkle stirring ominously in his chair, presumably about to uncurl and move into his 'Let's all stop talking drivel' mode. Fortunately perhaps, at that moment Josey knocked a paper cup half filled with water into his lap, and whatever he might have been intending to say was lost in a flurry of emergency drying activities. Josey appeared deeply upset by what she'd done, apologising sincerely and profusely, but then she turned and caught my eye. And winked.

Dennis, popping back from the Canaries for a flying visit, finished off the plenary session by thanking Anne and I for all our hard work, and said how much he'd enjoyed the 'Lightening the Bible' seminar yesterday afternoon. Could Gerald possibly treat us to a few more verses from the Gospel of Fidybus? Lips began to purse in a few quarters – but only a few. Gerald, of course, was more than happy to oblige. These were the extracts he read.

FIDYBUS 4:8-12

As Jesus and his disciples journeyeth towards Capernaum John saith, 'Oh, I say, Master, looketh thou over there. Seeth that stone, the one with the jagged bits that sticketh out on the left? Thinkest thou that on the other side it resembleth the profile of King Herod?'

Jesus sigheth and saith, 'Oh, not again. All right, let's have a look. No! This one looketh no more like Herod than the last four.'

'Oh,' saith John, 'well, I thinketh it doth. Andrew, what sayeth thou? Thinkest thou there existeth an faint suggestion of King Herod in yonder stone, or do I deceiveth mine self?'

'Thou deceiveth thyself,' answereth Andrew, and he refuseth to say any more or even look.

Then John calleth out in an loud voice, 'Oy! Thomas, Philip, draweth near to me and looketh at this rock from an particular angle.'

And Thomas muttereth under his breath, 'Here we go again, Phil. Verily this dolt hath an Herod fixation. Every single stone looketh like Herod to him. Mayhap he thinketh some loony sculptor goeth around carving every rock in sight into an likeness of the king.'

And Thomas and Philip putteth their hands over their mouths and staggereth about and giggleth immoderately until John departeth in an huff.

(FIDYBUS 14:9)
On a certain day Jesus yawneth, and Andrew saith unto him, 'Master, why yawneth thou?' And the Lord replieth, 'Sorry? Err . . . because I waxeth tired. Why mentioneth thou it?'

Andrew saith, 'Oh! Well, no reason – no, no, no, no . . .'

(FIDYBUS 17:4)
Behold, in the morning, an large crowd gathereth outside the house where the Master lodgeth, but the Lord was out, so they goeth away again.

(FIDYBUS 24:19-26)
Judas (not Iscariot) and Thomas, also known as Didymus, cometh to Jesus as he eateth an piece of broiled fish after an lengthy day in which he ministereth to many. Judas saith unto him, 'Master, sundry of us are not happy with our names. I myself, for instance, am weary of being negatively defined by being called Judas (*not Iscariot*). The thing is, Lord, that whensoever I am introduced to strangers, the

other disciples, whom I love, of course, maketh an point of saying, "Behold, Judas!" Then, as all draw their breath in sharply, these same disciples add, "Not Iscariot!" and falleth about laughing. Could I not henceforth be known as, something like, "Judas, the one who never betrayed anyone and says some rather interesting and original things from time to time?"'

Jesus replieth, 'If thou wilt just leave me to enjoy this last little piece of broiled fish, thou canst call thyself Elijah Trumpgirdle the Frog Balancer insomuch as it concerneth me.'

Thomas, also known as Didymus, saith, 'Quick word before we depart, Lord. As thou art aware, I am Thomas, also known as Didymus. *Didymus*, Master! I soundeth like an stuffed toy. An very small, squishy stuffed toy. Didymus! I soundeth like an stuff . . .'

Jesus saith, 'Verily I hear what thou art saying Thomas, and I think I can promise that in the age to come most will remember you by a quite different name. Believest thou that this will come to pass?'

'I doubt it.'

'Hmm! Anyway, I would like to finish my . . .'

Judas (not Iscariot) and Thomas, also known as Didymus, departeth, but as they departeth Judas saith, 'Oh, small point, Lord, two others waiteth outside to speak with thee on this subject.'

Jesus sigheth. 'And who mighteth they be?'

Judas (not Iscariot) saith, 'Er, one is she who is known as the Other Mary, Lord. The *Other* Mary. See? The other Mary? She faileth to understand why, being neither your mother nor the prostitute one nor the sister of Martha, she should not be known as "Mary, definitely never a prostitute and quite special in her own right." After all, Lord, when you thinketh about it . . .'

Jesus interrupteth, 'Look, just at the moment, all I desireth is to eat my dinner. Could you please just . . .'

'Forgive us, Lord. Yes! Behold, we departeth. Oh! Before I forget. The other person is thine own brother James, who hangeth about outside, too nervous to come in. You see, he feeleth uncomfortable about being known as "James the Less". It soundeth to him like "James the loser", or "James, the sad, spindly little weedy thing". He wondereth if thou wouldst vouch-safe that he be known henceforth as James the More. Or – or – or James the just as important as the other Jameses, even if he is a bit younger and marginally shorter.'

Jesus muttereth, 'Verily I might as well heal this fish and start all over again . . .'

Dennis said a prayer and we all (quite a lot of us) went a-hugging once more. Would have felt quite happy and a little bit proud if it hadn't been for the leaden weight at the bottom of my soul.

Polly Cluskey caught me in the corridor after the plenary session and asked if she could have a very quick word.

'I've had a wonderful weekend, Adrian,' she said. 'Thanks so much for organising it all. I felt so much more confident after Father John said those things, after the way the boys behaved during the silent meal. What was the idea behind that by the way? I wasn't quite sure at the time.'

I passed a finger around the inside of my collar.

'Ah, yes. Well, that was my idea, Polly, and not a very good one, I'm afraid. I read about it in a stupid book. It was supposed to be heart-warming and filled with grace and spiritual harmony and all that sort of thing, through the something-or-other soundless meeting of our eyes. I can't remember the precise wording in the book.'

She giggled and shook her head in wonder.

'The exact opposite of what happened, then.'

'Yes. I'm sorry. It was a bit of a disaster. I'm not saying silent meals don't have a place, but – well, this obviously wasn't it.'

'Oh, no, don't apologise. After all, if Eamonn and Patrick hadn't played up like they did Enid wouldn't have complained, and Father John wouldn't have said what he said, and Enid and I wouldn't be such good friends now. I'm going round to hers next week.'

She chewed her thumbnail for a moment.

'This is going to sound silly, but – do you think God sometimes uses these disastery sort of things to make something good happen?'

'There's not much hope for me if he doesn't, Polly.'

'Nor me! Anyway, what I actually wanted to say was that some of the mums and dads were talking about that weird Mussolini thing that old Mr Grimaldi did with the children earlier on. The thing with the lamppost.'

I shuddered.

'Yes.'

'Well, we weren't sure what to make of it. My Patrick was one of that group, so I asked him what he thought. He said, "Oh, Mum, that was my favourite bit of the whole weekend. Can we come back next year and hang another bad man from a lamppost?" I'm afraid I laughed. I know I shouldn't have, but I did. I told some of the other mums about that and most of them found it funny. And everyone understands that there were problems with the children's workers. After all, you didn't know what was going to happen yesterday, did you? Same with the two er – you know – the two women.'

'Mange and A rash?'

'Oh, goodness, yes! That was awful, wasn't it? That made me laugh as well, though. Anyway, Anne was brilliant the way she took over.'

She paused for an instant.

'Adrian, can I ask you one more question in case I don't get the chance later on?'

'Of course.'

'Well, it's been quite hard for me since Jason cleared off with his new "soul mate", and I suppose I've got a bit stressed and bothered about everything. Someone at church was trying to be helpful the other day. He said, "The thing is, Polly, despite everything, you can be sure that God loves you." Well, you know how it is. I nodded and agreed and all that, but I was thinking afterwards that God is no more hands-on than my ex-husband was. He doesn't take the rubbish out on a Monday night either. And what I wanted to ask you was this. When I was thinking that and chuckling to myself, I had the oddest feeling that God was laughing with me. It felt *so good*. You get into habits in your mind, don't you? I know I do. I've got into the habit of thinking that God is very serious and stern and watching me to make sure I don't do anything stupid or wrong. So, do you think he does laugh with me – with us? Does he like having a bit of fun sometimes?'

I don't often hug other women. I suppose I tend to assume that they've got better things to do with their personal space. It was just that Polly looked so tired and plaintive and hopeful and – nice.

'Yes, Polly,' I said into her right ear. 'I'm sure he's always looking for people to laugh with. And you've done so well with your boys. I reckon you and God both need someone to relax with from time to time.'

Eamonn and Patrick rushed up at that moment and hustled their mother away for their own very important homeward-bound purposes. Lovely family, but in need of someone to take a turn putting the rubbish out.

At about three o'clock Janice from the front desk found me to say that Father John was about to leave and wanted to say goodbye. Couldn't find Anne, so I went on my own. As I hurried out I wondered if this might be the last time I would see my friend in this world. Such a sad thought. Found him outside sitting like a dried-up bag of bones in the back of a big old car waiting to be driven away. Last chance for a last question.

Came out with some silly, ordinary things, then I said, 'Father John, I know this is a ridiculous question to ask as you're about to go, but could you just tell me – where do you think we can find the love of God?'

'Ah, you always have an easy one for me just before I push off, don't you?' he chuckled. 'I am so flattered that you think I might have any answers to a question like that. Actually, Adrian, people quite often want to know this kind of thing. Where is God? How do I perceive him? Where will I actually discover the love of God for myself? There are so many answers. Music, the Bible, the natural world, prayer and worship, poppies with a small and a capital "P", romantic love, Marilyn Monroe, kindness, all those things. All good and true answers in themselves. But, as I near the end of my life, what do I believe? I believe we need the courage, the humility and the sheer will to be able to say, "The only place where I can guarantee that you will find the love of God is in me." I personally have decided to do my best to be an aid-agency for the distribution of God's love to all who need it. But I am not responsible for supplies. As I give out, so my supplies seem to be replenished and replaced, and it is in the willingness to give out that I also experience the love of God in my life.

'Adrian, please, never forget that because of this we are so deeply indebted to those we serve. They are our generous benefactors. They are making us rich. In the meantime, I'm afraid there will be no great credit attached to this role. Each of us needs to be a sort of depot. We will have a delivery door at one side and a collection counter at the other. Amid all the truly impenetrable conundrums – those mysteries that remind us how the darkest and sharpest of shadows can be thrown by the brightest of lights – it might be almost as simple and as practical as that. The wages are good, though, or so I'm told. I shall know very soon. God bless you, Adrian, and your lovely wife, and Gerald, the best work you and Anne ever did, and the one who is leaning on you.'

The one who is leaning on me. How did he know? Perhaps she told him. Probably not. Wanted to ask him a question about Josey, but I was afraid that he might answer me.

As the car pulled away I heard Father John's thin, tired voice call out. I was barely able to catch his words over the noise of the engine.

'See you in Pizza Hut?'

Got away at last. All quite emotional, OK and not OK. Josey whispered in my ear just before they left, 'I'll send you a text in the morning after I've been to the doctor's. Sunshine for good. Rain for bad. But come anyway, won't you?'

Ran into Alan Varney in the hall just before leaving. Felt a bit uncomfortable about all our negative encounters. Shook his hand and said, 'Thanks, Alan, we really enjoyed our stay. I hope I didn't come over too – well, critical.'

'Hope is a spiritual imperative,' he replied, 'we look forward to your return.'

Not a flicker. Oh, well . . .

Quite late before Anne and I got home. Both exhausted.

I said to Anne, 'Oh, by the way, I forgot. Just before we left Josey asked if we could drive over tomorrow.'

'Really? We've only just left them. I could ring her now.'

'No, don't do that. She said she particularly wanted to talk to both of us about something. We'll find out what it is when we see her. Not a problem, is it?'

She yawned and shook her head at the same time. 'No, course not. I'm just glad they're not sick of us after forty-eight hours cheek to jowl.'

Into bed early. Before Anne dropped off I told her about my last conversation with Father John, and passed on his love.

'Oh, and he said that Gerald was the best work we ever did.'

Anne raised her head.

'Did he really say that?'

'Yes, he really did. Sleep well.'

'Yes, I think I'll be able to do that tonight.' She looked at me for a moment. 'Darling, there's nothing on your mind, is there? Nothing you should be telling me?'

'No,' I said lightly, turning my eyes away from her, 'honestly, there's nothing I should be telling you.'

Kissed her gently on the cheek.

'Good night.'

So wanted to ask her to stay awake with me. But I couldn't, could I? Not mine to tell. A small Gethsemane, but it really hurt. Lay awake in the dark, watching a pale strip of moonlight under the venetian blinds, and remembering some lines from a song I once heard.

> Whoever made days,
> Didn't make them right,
> All my days keep changing,
> Into weeping nights.

Monday's coming. Do what is required.

10

Monday Morning

At eleven o'clock this morning, just as we were about to leave, Anne picked my mobile phone up from the shelf by the front door where it was charging.

'There's a text,' she said, 'it's from Josey.'

Stood very still.

'What does it say?'

Anne shook her head.

'It doesn't say anything. Just a picture.'

'What sort of picture?'

'It's a rainbow. Any idea what that means?'

Took a deep breath.

'I hope so. Tell you on the way.'